transit

Library of Congress Cataloging-in-Publication Data

Share, Bernard.
Transit / Bernard Share. -- 1st ed.
    p. cm.
ISBN 978-1-56478-542-8 (pbk. : acid-free paper)
1. Time travel--Fiction. 2. Magic realism (Literature) 3. Ireland--Fiction.
I. Title.
PR6069.H335T73 2009
823'.914--dc22
                        2008050046

Partially funded by a grant from the Illinois Arts Council, a state agency,
and by the University of Illinois at Urbana-Champaign

www.dalkeyarchive.com

transit bernard share

Dalkey Archive Press ▣ Champaign and London

1

'Excuse me, but you're pissing on my foot.'

The man on the left, struggling with a white nightie, appeared to be about to burst into tears. But it was not the man on the left. And the voice had been . . . Embarrassed, and taking renewed aim, he looked down at the shoe, now shaking itself dry. A gesture and a brogue—must be going the other way. He still held the yellow card in his left hand, and this, coupled with the restraint of the overnight bag on his shoulder *(Please take all your personal belongings with you)* had contributed to the misdemeanour.

'Sorry,' he said, still looking at the shoe, now rubbing itself inconsequentially against the back of the right leg of the heavy trousers. 'A stream of near-unconsciousness, I'm afraid.' His tongue curled comfortably around the words—it had been some time since he had spoken in polysyllables.

'Think nothing of it. And you're . . . ?'

'On the KLM,' he said, deliberately offering the wrong answer. Concentrating on the one-handed disposal of the last drops, he had not yet looked at the face. The voice spoke of old-school ties. He glanced again at the greasy card in his right hand and saw that the man in the nightie, having apparently restored himself to perfect modesty, was looking at it too.

'I almost wasn't going to get off,' he said to the man on the right, who was rezipping the heavy trousers as if inhuming a family treasure. 'But you know how it is, anything to stretch the legs. And all those little men who invade you with dustpans and brushes, hands one way, eyes targeting valuables like . . . ' But he couldn't locate a simile.

'. . . invaders from another time zone,' said the man on the right, now combing sparse hair. 'They've just had an early breakfast, whereas you . . . what have you just had?'

'I skipped the last one, whatever it was. There were crossed-out pigs. For the Moslems. I didn't fancy them, somehow.'

'I know what you mean. I'm still ruminating on the black pudding, sausages and champagne. But haven't we . . . ?'

'Oh, all the time in the world, I should imagine. They said an hour, but you can probably double that. What time is it?'

The other looked at his watch. 'Two A.M. And you?'

'About nine in the morning, I should think. But mine's stopped. Automatic, don't you know. I'm not sure what day. And here?'

'God only knows. Shall we . . . ?'

And there's another thing, he thought, as they left more or less together, still unwilling to embark upon an intimacy that might be prolonged beyond reasonable expectation by the yellow cards. 'Mine's blue,' the man on the right had said, 'but I suppose it means the same thing—gritty coffee and a goat sandwich.' And there's another thing, he was still thinking, though a little late now to be apposite: here at least the jacks smell like jacks, good honest piss and that kind of disinfectant that, Jaysus, went out with the aerosols. Like the smell used to be out the back door of a bonafide.

'Mine's blue,' the other had said, not even bothering to check it. 'But I suppose it means the same thing. Gritty coffee and a . . .'

'If indeed the restaurant, or whatever it is, is functioning. What time did you say it was?'

'Here? I've no idea. I keep the watch on what used to be GMT until I get there. One short, sharp shock. Could be breakfast. Gritty coffee and a toasted goat sandwich. Where are we, anyway? I mean which of them? Not that it matters.'

They walked past gates 7, 6, 5, 4, bundles of nightied figures like laundry dumped outside hotel rooms. Isn't this the one where you walk in a circle, past gates 6, 5, 4, the crumpled, snoring soldiers, the minimal duty-free, the soft drinks bar, the transfer desk, always untenanted, the bookstall (backward Arabic romances on jacks paper), gates 6, 5, 4, the crumpled, snoring soldiers, the minimal duty-free, the soft . . .

They walked it twice, neither inclined to make the suggestion to seek the restaurant, possibly, possibly not, on the floor above, where they might have to sit and face one another, inaugurating something other than an ambulatory association.

'At least it stretches the legs.' From the careful banality of the remark he knew that the other was trying to place him, riffling through dusty card-indexes. 'That's the last Irishman left in College: we don't know how he got in.' No. 'Wee Clow, an Ulster existentialist.' No. 'Clontarf Vikings versus Belgrove at Mount Prospect.' Hardly. Were they even working on the same files?

On the third circuit they stopped, as if by mutual agreement, at the head of the stair—unregarded on the first two rounds—that led down to the passport, baggage and exit area. But at these stop-overs nobody ever left. Perhaps if they were to try? A glacial refusal, an insistence on an unprocurable visa, a currency form to be completed in Amharic. They stood staring down at a lounging guard at the bottom of the stairs whose evident boredom seemed the more completely to compromise the freedom to walk through a door.

'In Amsterdam, between planes,' said the other, still looking down, 'I sometimes take the train into town. The toy shop in the walking street, the girls behind the glass—though it always seems too early even were I that way inclined. The armchair is empty and she's out the back ironing her . . .'

'Amsterdam.' Gratefully, he took it up. 'My last time was very early in the morning—their time. I got caught up in the tide of commuters flooding out of Central Station. Pinched, resigned faces. I wanted to tell them I'd just lived through half the day they were facing and that it wasn't going to be that bad. But of course . . .' he trailed off, embarrassed.

'Do you think this would rate a beer?' The other was peering dubiously at his blue ticket. 'Or at least something not actively offensive to drink? I'd be willing to forego the sandwich.'

They had joined a group milling like disturbed woodlice at another stairs—ascending this time—amongst whom he recognised, and quickly tried to unrecognise, some formerly contiguous fellow-passengers. Not like the old days by sea. Straitjacket seats and high-chair meals, nursery talk with the boy next door. Maybe years ago a chance encounter, a snuggle under a blanket, a suspender . . . he flushed guiltily, dirty old man, remembering the old roll of undeveloped film he had found when packing up to go and handed to the lab boy, taking the risk it might have been anything, anyone, anywhere, someone with no clothes on. He looked at the man now mounting the steps in front of him: about his own age, balding ditto but less paunchy, going, as he had observed, the other way—thin, pale face and thick, dark trousers the testimony—government or semi-state, perhaps even in the same line of business. He'd been away too long. Wee Clow, the Ulster existentialist? The nickname came back without its validating substance. Long ago.

Whatever mealtime it was, the restaurant was less than prepared for it. A waiter who looked as if he had been recently exhumed from a downstairs pile of dirty washing thrust a detumescent card at them on which were listed half a dozen hazardous approximations of culinary reality: *sope of the days; mustered shrump stick poms; garden pee.* On being shown the yellow and blue cards, he shrugged indifferently: if they implied a subtle difference in status, nothing in his lack of demeanour betrayed it.

'Drink,' said the other, the hand assuming the long-radius curve appropriate to the encircling of a pint.

The waiter waved economically, a movement barely qualifying as a gesture, towards a corner in which a number of bottles stood on a table, the infiltered dust of the desert lending them what was almost certainly an undeserved patina of age.

'Shall we investigate?'

He followed him without much enthusiasm over to what proved to be a minimal if eclectic wine-cellar. They agreed that, given the location, the most negotiable for a piece of blue or yellow cardboard was likely to be the Jordanian claret. He watched the other walk over with it to the sleepy cashier. Was everyone here sleepy all the time, like an undeveloped fairy tale—someday my prints? Did they all just drop where they stood when the last jumbo of the day or night or whatever lumbered into the sky? He watched him as he entered into negotiation with the air of a man who had done it all before, not quite putting the natives in their place, one didn't think like that these bilateral days, or pretended not to, hoping for a clue that would enable him . . . That evening in College with the Pope in full spate in No. 28: 'Brendan Bracken, Sir Sydney Luytens, Churchill, Patricia Hutchens, the editor of the *Meath Chronicle*.' The unlikely names had lodged themselves into a litany over the years. But who else had been there? In the flesh? Your man?

No. Nothing reverberated. He was searching for a name for which he had forgotten the mnemonic. As the tall, slightly stooping figure turned, a small smile of triumph at having won something for nothing, he tried to invest him with identity of dim contemporaries cod-acting in Front Square, kicking Hoare's loaf (whatever happened to the well-bred, pun-burdened Hoare?) into a tree. Still too far down the pile: all he came up with was the familiar random sequence of snapshots, fruit of too much travel to too many places in too little time—places he often had no recollection of ever having seen. He had often been perturbed by this apparently unassociated recall, but felt that to describe it to others would be to lay boastful claim to spatial conquests. That character it must have been '48 who came back from the long vacation with stories of having flown into Berlin with the airlift. Who was *he*?

But even if that name wouldn't come he could see nothing in his present companion of the Portadown (he recalled, at least, the provenance) thin-faced chancer whose succeeding sexual anecdotes, when all the sensation had been milked out of the Berlin non-episode, aroused furtive longings in his recently-schoolboy hearers who had yet to touch the hem of a garment: and with the

New Look that would not have got us very far. And as the bottle was placed between them, label turned in his direction, calling, he supposed, for some oenological observation that would stand in for the toast that neither of them was, he sensed, prepared to offer . . . But why? Surely the easiest thing in the world, and the most natural to say, pouring ('I'll be mammy'): it must be all of forty years but weren't you around in my time? I certainly have the feeling we have met before though to be honest . . .

To be honest was the difficulty. Too many recent and less recent defensive deployments, covering up for colleagues unable to make the readjustment from foreign postings, Bonaire to Baldoyle, or for himself, delayed at the office dear with one hand clasping . . .

A hand appeared from somewhere over his right shoulder holding what appeared to be an offensive weapon—well at least, he thought irrationally, it's not a hijack—but which resolved itself (he had taken off his glasses the better not to see his opposite number) into a corkscrew. The waiter, having observed the transaction with the blue ticket, clearly now regarded them both as bonafide. This time he mentally enunciated it, out of its pub context, with the Latin inflexion: *oculi omnium in te sperant Domine, tu das iis escam eorum.*

'*In tempore opportuno,*' he said aloud, wishing now that he had his glasses on, but the other made no marginally-visible response. If Trinity, then living out of College, or a graceless medical.

'It's one of those things that transports you back in time, as Bernadette Comerford said the other morning about the singing of Kirsten Flagstad.'

'Sorry, I'm not with you.'

'No, of course, I suppose you haven't been home for some time. A morning radio programme.'

'Oh yes. But I wouldn't have thought that Jordanian claret . . .'

'No, not the wine. This encounter.' Through the myopia he could sense the eyes piercing him. 'It must be all of forty years but weren't you around in my time? I certainly have the feeling that we . . .'

A loudspeaker on the wall above them came alive with a crack like a burst from a pump-action corkscrew *ATTENTION PAS-SENGERS, ATTENTION PASSENGERS. THIS IS AN IMPOR-TANT ANNOU* and subsided, prematurely, with a corroded-ter-minal rattle. They waited in silence, as did the scattering of fel-low-travellers, for a resumption. None was forthcoming.

'Anyway, your good health. Sláinte.' As if the question had been satisfactorily settled between them. His sip of cautious ap-praisal was almost turned into total immersion by the sudden immanence of the waiter, face this time grinning, teeth like the old piano in No. 4, and a plateful, tastelessly arranged, of the goat sandwiches.

'Should we tip him?'

'With what?' In the wallet in the overnight bag there were, possibly, a few stray American dollars, an Irish pound, old green Kathleen Mavourneen style, that he had carried since College. Maybe a birr or two.

'You know Ethiopia?'

The other nodded, as if being accused of ignorance of the Rubrics.

'I always wanted to try and buy a pint with one in County Of-faly, just for pig-iron. Birrs, don't you know.'

'I did. Once. A pub in the back of beyond—Kilcormac or somewhere out that way, buried in the bog. Thought I was the great fellow, but as I was about to hand it over, accidentally on purpose, didn't I see the boss had one pinned up over the bar together with the usual concatenation of francs, lire, pesetas and so forth. Everyone's been everywhere these days.'

'And yourself?' It could go either way.

'Oh yes, off again, probably the last stint, and in a way I won't be sorry. Only I will, you know. It's the parochialism that gets to me—not the parochialism of Ireland, that's endemic—but that of our particular corner of the globe. Over-cosy. Something to do, I suppose, with always having Christmas in winter.'

'Well, bon voyage anyway. Wherever it is.'

'And safe home. Presuming that either of us is ever permitted to get up and go. How long are we here?'

The restaurant clock was stopped at two something, the big hand missing. Time was calibrated only by the level of the wine, an unreliable red shift. The hand opposite him was running quavers up and down the glass.

'Do you play?' He nodded at the uncompleted cadenza.

'That's a funny thing. The only time I was picked for the first eleven it was too late to include my name on the list. So I appeared under the common mantle. *A N Other*. It wasn't that I was any great shakes—never, in fact, played again at that level. But for some reason it stuck. For a couple of terms I was known just as Other. We were still the next best thing to schoolboys after all.'

'It was the style, of course. Surnames. Or as you were listed in the Calendar, all embarrassing middle names revealed. *Dillon, Barbara Agnes; Smythe, Basil Courtney* . . . marmoreal, chisellers' stuff. Then again you sometimes never knew the Christian name, whereas nowadays . . . Al, meet Col. Col, meet . . .'

The bottle was nearly empty. 'I wonder. My yellow ticket?'

'Worth a try. It's wojous, but what else is one to do. Go and wave it at your man while I attend, if you will excuse me, to a call of . . .'

He was halfway to the wine counter, moving, he noted with rather indignant surprise, somewhat unsteadily. The remaining labels were a blur, only marginally resolving themselves when he put on his glasses. It seemed safest, bureaucratically speaking, to stick to the Jordanian, of which there remained two or three bottles. He selected one—they were all of the same unilluminating year—and carried it over to the waiter who was now doubling as cashier. He was proffering the yellow card when he felt a hand on his shoulder. It was A N Other, his face . . .

'You're as white as a sheik.' They were seated once more with a bottle between them, but the crude attempt at levity appeared lost. 'You're sure you're all right?' he asked. 'Perhaps the . . .'

'Game ball,' said Other, swallowing half a glass. 'I've had a bad fright, that's all. The jacks . . .'

'More than usually odiferous?'

'It's not that. Look, there's no reason why you should want to become involved.'

'Go on.'

'But I've just had a very strange experience. Would you mind very much coming to the jacks with me? The cubicle?'

'It will look rather peculiar, wouldn't you think?'

The smile was strained. 'Nothing like that, I assure you. Not even ambidextrous.'

On a train pulling out of Templemore. You go first, lock the door. I'll knock four times, like this. They had managed it with her bending over the wash-hand basin, the warning on the wall *FOGRA: NUAIR BHIONN AN BOD ISTIGH SA* . . . Steam of course in those days. At the moment of truth he had put his foot on the thing that flushed the water.

'You go first then. And lock the door. I'll knock four times. Like this. But really . . .'

'I'm very grateful to you. It may be nothing. But I need another pair of eyes.'

'Jet-lagged and astigmatised by Jordanian plonk like your own. Before you go . . .' he raised his glass in the toast he had thus far studiously avoided: 'To old times.'

'If you don't mind,' said A N Other, 'I'd rather not drink to that.' He drank.

2

At first he thought he had taken a wrong turn and wandered into the Ladies'—both pictograms, not unreasonably, wore Arab-length garments clothing their indeterminate outline. But what he at first took to be a clean knickers dispenser on the wall (still distancing reality by not wearing the glasses) revealed itself as a supererogatory appliance designed to blow hot air, or perhaps, according to prevailing conditions, CS gas. The Gents', for such it proclaimed itself by the vertical plumbing, was sparingly ap-pointed. Apart from the four contiguous stalls, there were two cubicle doors, both of them shut.

Knock four times and disturb the chief of police, or a stool pigeon. He couldn't bring himself to call out the nickname, even sotto voce. And a whispered 'is it yourself, man of the house?' might still draw the wrong card. He listened for sounds, anything bordering on farts, indicating serious purpose rather than a waiting game. To be caught attempting to peer under the door with the intention of identifying A N Other by a prominent brogue might prove equally difficult to laugh off. But then there was a cough from the right-hand compartment, familiar enough for him to decide to chance it. He knocked four times.

The door opened instantly, as if Other's fingers had been al-ready on the latch. As nonchalantly as possible—though the customary mode of entering a gents' toilet at that point eluded him—he went in, closing the door behind him, swinging over the gnawed chrome handle to secure the conventional privacy.

The first thing he noticed was that Other's brow, of necessity no great distance from his own, was marbled in sweat. The next, that this was the most idiosyncratic cubicle that he could recall having encountered. Instead of the conventional layout—door facing onto bowl, cistern and other accoutrements—the plumbing sat on a lateral wall. Facing him, as he stood with his back to the door he had just entered, was another door. A jacks with a jacks en suite?

'I opened it,' said A N Other, his voice little above a gargle.

'And?'

'You will have to see for yourself. If there is anything to see.'

There was something in his manner that discouraged further questions. In spite of the heat there was a cold crepitation at the back of his neck such as he had experienced only once before, all those years ago in College when on a still summer evening he thought he had heard a ghost writer typing away in the vacated rooms beside him.

'All right,' he said, knowing that if he didn't make the move then and there, he never would. He took the two or three short paces over to the opposing door, A N Other shrinking himself to the side wall to permit his progress, and swinging over a replicated chrome handle, opened it. It was another jacks. He turned, voice unsteady with relief.

'Another jacks. Unusual, I admit, but nothing, I would have thought, to get excited about. They open it, I suppose, to cope with a sudden flow of . . .'

He stopped. It was a jacks, certainly, but there was something not right about it. First of all, it was in almost total darkness.

Secondly, it stank—even by the standards of the one in which they were standing (neither had moved to cross the threshold). Thirdly, there was a figure pissing against the wall, which seemed to serve the purpose of urinal, who, if he had seen them, gave no sign of acknowledging their presence. As they stood watching him, he finished his business, turned and disappeared through a dark gap at the far end which did not appear to frame a door.

'Did you see that?' asked A N Other.

'Your man? Yes, of course.'

'Did you see what he was doing?'

'Pissing. Like you or me, or, saving your presence, any other . . .'

'No, not that.'

'What?'

'He buttoned his flies.'

'So? Maybe old habits wear longer in this part of the . . .' But then he realised; the clothes were all wrong. The stance—something about the stance. The smell—no perfume of Arabia.

'I see what you mean.'

'Do you? When I looked in here first—pure curiosity, of course—there were two of them. They were talking English.'

'People do. The other door probably leads to . . .'

'They were talking about the declaration of the Irish Republic in 1949.'

'An unrewarding subject of conversation, I would admit, but not . . .'

'They were talking about it as if it had happened yesterday.'

'I see.' But he didn't. He looked out across the threshold, which both of them were taking some care not to cross, into the now deserted jacks. The splarge dripped water into the clogged gutter.

From where they stood they could sense the chill in the air. A familiar damp.

'It's one of those things that transports you back . . .'

'I don't believe in that class of thing,' interrupted A N Other. 'Science fiction, time wefts or whatever you call them.'

'No more do I. You probably misheard them. After all, the jet-lag, not to mention . . .'

'I'm only eight hours or so on the move.'

'The wine. Not the best.' But he wasn't even convincing himself.

'We could go and look,' said A N Other.

'Where?'

'Out the far door.'

But as they stood staring at one another, neither prepared to make the first move, there was a shuffling of feet on what sounded like wet gravel and a hunched figure staggered rather than walked through the black space at the far end of the contiguous jacks, eddying inconclusively towards the suppurating black wall. He was wearing a thick suit, a collarless shirt with a gold stud and a battered trilby hat. Cowherd, he concluded irrationally: Swineherd? Potsherd?

'Buttons again,' said A N Other.

'*So tired,*' sang, or quavered the figure in a heavy tenor, '*of dreaming of you; so tired . . .*' The voice slid off the note like a tepid knife off dripping, submerging under the urine obbligato.

'Russ Morgan? Russ Conway?'

'You know him?' asked Other.

'No: the song. One of those things. The Irish Hospitals Sweepstakes Goodwill Musical Hour . . .'

He realised suddenly that they were talking, though in low voices, as if aurally insulated from the pissing figure—as indeed they seemed to be. He neither looked in their direction nor acknowledged them in terms of adopting the hunched, protective stance of the pisser observed.

'*So tired . . .*' The empty interval dwindled into the scrunch of gravel.

'It's now or never,' he said with a confidence he did not feel, 'before anyone else appears. Let's just take a look out that far door and get back to the wine. What do you say?'

'They might have called the flights.'

'If crossed-out pigs had wings.'

'What did they call you in College?' asked A N Other unexpectedly, his half-raised brogue poised over the threshold.

'I never ran to a nickname—at least not as far as I was aware. When I used to write the odd time for the *Miscellany* I signed myself Meniscus . . . pseudonyms were the thing, if you remember, and most of them were in Latin: Discus, Pentax, Domestos . . .'

'Meniscus,' said Other, 'slightly over the top, but it will do. Come on.'

3

'The conventional Irish pub scene,' said A N Other.

The potsherd had, on regaining his customary position behind the bar, removed the hat and was in the early stages of pulling a pint when the two quare hoors, as he was later to categorise them, came in from the door leading out up the yard to the Gents'. In the normal way (it was half an hour to closing and pressure was building to the last orders) he would have paid them little heed, except that he did not recall having seen them enter the premises. And the way your man was dressed, the short, fat one: a get-up you'd see on Dollymount Strand or some class of a tennis court rather than . . .

'But where?'

'Never mind where for the moment. We'll have to put up or shut up. If you follow me. The recognised practice upon entering licensed premises is to order a drink. Failure to embark upon that course lays one open to a variety of imputations. The difficulty resides in the fact . . .'

'The money.'

'Precisely. Assume we are victims of some kind of temporal delusion . . .'

'Kathleen Comerford?'

'More or less. It could reasonably be assumed, judging by the general appearance of the premises, that we have been transported backward; though, by the look of it, not very far.'

'I always thought of this class of thing as involving centuries: H G Wells, don't you know.'

'Seemingly there is the small-scale, bargain variety also. Which might suggest that . . .'

'I have a pound.'

They had been standing, more or less instinctively, at a point and in a manner calculated to suggest that they were simply delaying the advance to the bar and the placing of an order whilst they settled some small point of procedure involving, perhaps, the prerogative of paying for the round or the advisability of delaying until the arrival of bosom companions even now disgorging themselves from battered Anglias in the vicinity. He unzipped the overnight bag, which he was wearing slightly off the shoulder (would you look at your man with the lady's handbag, he almost heard someone say) and extracted his wallet, from which he removed the green £1 Nota Dlí-Thairgthe which he had held onto, for reasons not entirely clear to him, all these years. Through the oval porthole on the left, Lady Lavery regarded him coolly. The date in the bottom right-hand corner read 30.3.48.

'We're made up. This should get us two pints and no questions asked. I suggest that you, Other, as the more conventional in appearance, do the honours. Here.'

He handed over the note (not without the feeling of parting from an old friend) and, with the intention of rendering himself as inconspicuous as possible, slid into a corner beside a somewhat scholarly-looking individual reading a folded newspaper which, from its typography and layout, suggested a 1950s *Irish Times*. Without the glasses he could make little of it; but, screwing up his eyes, he managed to bring into focus a portion of a centre column:

> . . . had established themselves in a modest jewellery and horological business in Clanbrassil Street. Chapman had left the counter upon some pretext—Keats, who liked on occasions to affect nautical terminology, was later to maintain that he had failed to keep his watch— when a small girl entered the premises proffering for their professional attention a timepiece of respectable appearance and apparently, to the attuned ear, regular chronometric function though deficient in the matter of a minute hand. At that moment Keats felt the necessity to respond to a call of nature, an imperative which fortunately coincided with the return of Chapman from his unexplained mission to the rere of the premises. 'Ah, Chapman,' said Keats, already making tracks for the door: 'Would you give the little lady a big . . .'

'There we are.' An unfocussed pint on the rickety table in front of him. 'And your change.'

He looked at the heap of heavy coins A N Other was placing in his palm, nestling in an orange ten-shilling note the soggy texture of which proclaimed its pub provenance. It takes you back, he was about to say . . .

'Oh a quare pair all right. Well-spoken and all that, your man, but didn't seem to know the price of a pint and as for the other one over there in the fancy dress trying to get a screw at Mr O's paper . . .'

'Did you get a clue?' asked A N Other.

'I couldn't very well put on the glasses and lean over. Let's just drink up quietly and go.'

'If we're not on a one-way ticket. What happens when the flights are called in our absence?'

'Unless of course in a manner of speaking we are still . . .'

'Look in the mirror,' said A N Other, 'I noticed it coming over with the pints.'

He got up on a pretext of searching for something he had let fall under the table and glanced into the gilded glass hanging over their heads. Behind the legend LOCKE'S PURE POT STILL WHISKEY, the bar and its customers appeared with something approaching normal fidelity. The only missing reflection was himself.

'I see what you mean,' he said, resuming his seat, 'or rather I don't see.'

'Look at your watch.'

'It's stopped. As I told you.'

'Mine too. And it was working perfectly.'

'But the pub clock appears to be going. Half-eleven. If this is the kind of place I think it is they close—used to close—at twelve. And we can't decently leave before then without attracting unwelcome attention. In the meantime, act naturally and avoid clichés.'

'Clichés?'

'Your man with the paper. All ears. And I got the date when he refolded it there: Tuesday April 19, 1949. So watch your language: nothing about grass roots growing up through the shop floor at this moment in time, that class of thing. No parameters.'

'Let's face it?'

'Not as far as I remember. Across the board was the chess column. Summits were still the tops of mountains. Packages had string.'

'Are you sure?' asked A N Other.

'No, I'm not at all sure. I caught a glimpse of the headline. Something about the GPO and guns.'

'But that was 1916.'

'Remember the conversation you thought you heard? The declaration of the Republic in 1949 was marked by a discharge of guns at the GPO on the Sunday night, I was in rooms in College, working for some exam. Went out to see the non-celebrations and didn't sleep till four.'

'And where might you have been a couple of nights after?' asked A N Other, 'tonight, as it were?'

'The next day was Easter Monday. The exam would probably have started the day after, or thereabouts. Probably still working. I always left it to the last minute.'

'No chance you would have been out drinking? In a bonafide? Matt Smith's, for instance?'

'Absolutely none. A Saturday night during term, perhaps—if there was anyone with a car.'

'We'll be spared that, anyway,' said A N Other with obvious relief.

'I'm not with you.'

'No, you wouldn't have been.'

'What are you suggesting?'

'No reflection,' said A N Other hastily, 'I think another pair of pints are in order. You might perhaps initiate a little conversation with our friend—find out at least where we are.'

'Or who we are. It's fifteen minutes to closing time, give or take. We've all the time in the world. I don't remember the bonafides being all that eager to put you out the door. Unless of course the Guards . . .'

'The last thing we need. At the first sight of a size eleven boot, out with us to the jacks.'

'Together with three dozen others intent on avoiding having their false names taken? We walk through the door and lead them all like a pair of pie-eyed pipers to the pleasure of the Jordanian . . .'

'Would you ever order the pints, like a decent man?'

He had been dreading the moment when he would have to approach the bar counter and its whey-faced, single-studded attendant.

'Two pints. When you're ready.' He opted for the coda as having some ring of timeless verisimilitude, though he could not recall having—the impatience of youth—employed it as a student when anyway he drank bottles. The overnight bag he had left on the seat behind him, so that the open-necked, short-sleeved shirt, apart from being fabricated from material probably not yet invented (dralon? cuprinol? crimplene?) denoted him as, perhaps, no more than a mild eccentric. But the suntan . . . he glanced at the mirror behind the bar and quickly glanced away again. It would take time to get used to not being there.

Apart from the fact that the beer handles were functional and the big, brass National cash register was reading 8s 11d (an expansive round somewhere), there was little to distinguish the premises, temporally speaking, from what might have been a country pub—or what he was remembering, after the years of absence, as a country pub—in what he was still thinking of as the present.

But then they had yet to gut the Victorian interiors, fit them out with genuine plastic, and refit them again in fake Victorian. The boss was staring at him, disconcerted, he realised, more by his silence than his appearance of obvious exile.

'Not a bad class of a day. For the time of year that's in it.' That's safe enough, surely.

'We can't complain.' A pause as the head was built. 'You were up for the match?'

Oh no. He tried to focus on a random printout of fixture lists. Triple Crown? We won it, didn't we, around then . . . now? Tom Clifford the dustman, now cleansing operative. Strathdee and Kyle. Or the hurling final? Never knew the first thing about the game and cared less, wrong tradition. Not soccer, surely? With your Drums and Bohs and Drums and Bohs . . .

'No, more's the pity' (and that didn't sound right). 'On our way to town, as it happens.' (But supposing this is Mullinahone, Ballydehob, Two-Mile-Borris?) 'One or two for the road.' The accent, still Trinity protestant after all the absent years, would fix him as a stranger, help him, with any luck, to keep his distance. The pints came up and he succeeded in paying relatively unself-consciously, sliding a half-crown into a stout-puddle, only glancing at the change.

Mr O was watching him over the top of 'An Irishman's Diary,' glasses half-way down the nose. Blow-ins, brought over by that new crowd Fógra Fáilte, there's bog Irish for you, to learn the art of minding mice through the medium. He had refolded the paper once more. The taller one, seated in the corner on his right, was trying to read it over his shoulder whilst pretending to be absorbed in the opposite wall. As the fat one approached, glasses halfway down, he slammed the *Times* onto his knee, barely averting a spillage as it caught the edge of the bockety table.

'Stranger in these parts, if you don't mind my asking?'

'In a manner of speaking. It's been a long time.'

'A travelling man?'

'Worked abroad, yes. In fact we're only off the boat this morning—Cobh, don't you know.'

'All round the world for sport,' said Mr O, half to himself. Your man must be petrified in that tennis outfit, and at his age too. He accepted, with barely a show of reluctance, the offer of something similar. 'In that case,' he said, 'a small Power. Your watch is stopped.'

'Yes indeed,' said the tennis-player, glancing at it nervously. 'And I've had no trouble at all with it since I bought it in Weir's of Dublin, or was it West's, in nineteen fif . . .' he broke off, apparently the victim of some inner confusion.

'Nineteen and fifteen? It owes you nothing, so. Though if you were to ask me I would have said that it was one of those modern self-winding yokes, incablocs and all.'

'You're in the watchmaking business?' asked the taller man.

'I have what you might describe as a passing interest. Did you know there was an alarm clock made in the seventeenth century would light a candle for you from a bit of tinder at any hour of the day or night you cared to name? Would have come in handy last night, that's for sure. I was reading'—here he tapped the paper—'about the eclipse and the way the dogs set up a long line of lamentation stretching from here to Mullingar, one taking up from the other. I suppose you'd scarcely have seen it and you on the high seas?'

'May I look at the account?' asked the tennis-player. Mr O passed him the *Times,* jabbing a paragraph with an almost steady finger. 'But this isn't today's paper?'

'And why would it be today's paper?' He leaned over, recoiling slightly at the poncy smell off the tennis-player's neck, and jabbed the finger again: 'There you are. Thursday April 14, 1949 . . .'

'But the Republic celebrations?'

'Sure that isn't till Sunday. If celebrations is the right word for it. Half-a-dozen English Spitfires and a few oul' guns couldn't hit Liberty Hall at twenty yards. Dev was right to have nothing to do with it. You heard about it, and you still all at sea?'

'But that was nineteen . . . I mean this is nineteen . . .'

'Nineteen and forty-nine. You don't mean to tell me that wherever it was you came from . . . ?'

'Of course not,' said the bigger man hurriedly. 'And now, if you'll excuse us, we'd better be making tracks.'

'You'll have one for the road surely?'

'Another time perhaps,' said the tennis-player, 'we'll get you again.'

Mr O did not appear to take this in good part. The eyes over the glasses, one left unfinished, glittered with mild malice. 'I can see through you. I can see through both of you.'

'Now, Mr O,' said the boss, who had sidled up, garnering empties, winking in the tobacco fug, 'there's no call for that. I'm sure these gentlemen . . .'

'I can see through them, I tell you. As sure as you're standing there, Matt, as large as life and twice as contrary.'

'The jacks?' said the tennis-player.

'Out the back and straight across,' said the boss. 'But surely you know that already.'

'Yes, indeed,' said the bigger man, 'if you will excuse us.'

The door had gone.

'What do we do now?'

'Piss,' said A N Other, 'there's somebody coming.'

Up against the wall they sensed rather than saw a shuffling figure line up beside them, waited, doing their best to feign full bladders, until he had buttoned up and gone.

'Now,' said A N Other, 'perhaps if we walk slowly in the direction . . .'

But the door was there. The chrome handle yielded solidly to the touch. 'A trick of the light,' he said. Over the threshold they were once more in the airside accommodation with—he immediately tested it—the far door still secure. 'Jaysus.' A N Other collapsed onto the unlidded seat: 'A close-run thing.'

'Why did you come up with all that guff about Cobh? I nearly put my foot in it.'

'I had to say something. It was at least some kind of alibi.'

'Did he see through us?'

'He'll put it down to the jigs in the morning. I was more worried about the others.'

'The others?'

'There were a couple of faces I thought I recognised. I was smoothing out wrinkles, correcting stoops, putting hair back on people I'd buried only recently—near-contemporaries, half-acquaintances . . . you know the sort of thing. The dwindling Prods. You feel, certainly in the country, you have to pay the last respects, even if it's someone you hardly knew and never liked. But then you've been away. Come on.' He got up, stuck out a bony, tweeded behind. 'Am I marked for life? A hint of a lunulus?'

'Nothing visible.'

'*Arse est celare* . . . all right, back to reality.'

'Which way?'

4

'It would have been nice to have been able to turn on a radio,' said A N Other.

'Wireless. Jack Jackson's "Record Round-Up." Life gets tedious, don't it? A Carnival Special in Cafolla's, when we could run to it. Kids in the street playing pat-the-baker. It all comes back to you.'

'It doesn't.'

Exiting severally, they had found the half-empty bottle of wine on the table undisturbed, the single stopped hand of the clock still pointing to somewhere about two. Nothing else seemed to have changed.

'It doesn't,' reiterated A N Other. 'What's this you said the pseudonym was again?'

'Meniscus.'

'I'll abjure my natural predilection and call you Rimmer. That wine tastes even worse than before, if that were possible. But it doesn't.'

'Doesn't what?'

'All come back to you.'

ATTENTION PASSENGERS THIS IS AN IMPORTANT ANNOU

'What do you mean it doesn't all come back to you?'

'The newspaper,' said A N Other. 'That was the giveaway. We were both presumably—I know I was—casting around for verifiable detail. How much can you really remember about Sunday, April the 17th, 1949?'

'I was working, as I told you, for some exam.'

'What exam?'

'Term? Schol? Mod? Little-Go? Not the remotest recollection.' All so agonisingly discrete at the time, long since congealed into one huge unanswerable question. *Life gets tedious, don't it? Discuss.* 'I had tried to work through the celebrations, given up, gone out, milled around with the vastly unimpressed crowd in O'Connell Street ironically cheering the popgun salute. At least I presumed irony at the time, a republic declared in a fit of pique by the party elected to uphold the Commonwealth connection. Couldn't sleep afterwards.'

'That's not bad for a start.'

'And probably not entirely on account of the guns. I had almost certainly had a lady to tea. *The Junior Dean presents his compliments and grants you permission to entertain Miss . . .*'

'You were in rooms?'

'The Rubrics. I would have met her at Front Gate at three. By half-three, maybe a little later, we would have been in the armchair. Snogging, I suppose we would have called it. All so unimaginably different and all so long ago. MacNeice? Or maybe Eliot?'

'The Euminides and Davy Arthur,' suggested A N Other.

'You were Mod. Lang.?' asked Rimmer.

'Classics. You must have noticed me wincing at your pronunciation of the Grace.'

'You were the boys in the blue suits. Perfect quantities. Certain of your opinions and only too ready to offer them at every verse end. *If I had to make the choice I'd prefer the Tower of Babel to the sound of Rothwell's voice talking at the Commons table.*'

'What was that?'

'One of those things that transports you back. That bottle's nearly dead. Shall we . . . ?'

'As I was saying about the newspaper,' said A N Other, 'in changing its dates it was doing no more than mirror . . '

'That bit I didn't like. I've never trusted them. But to see yourself not there.'

'We'll come to that. But the changing *Times* was merely reflecting, if you will forgive me, our inability accurately to relocate ourselves.'

'Which is why he saw through us?'

'Please?' It was the barman-cashier-waiter, holding up a bottle with what might have been a smile on his face, had he had the teeth to define it.

'I suppose so,' said A N Other, 'though I imagine that now it's for money.' But the man waved away both an offered credit card and Rimmer's rustic birr.

'A bad sign,' said Other, 'it means that the establishment is anticipating the pleasure of our company for some time to come.'

'On the other hand . . '

'Unfinished business?'

'I wouldn't mind another look,' said Rimmer, 'at least it would fill in the time.'

'It wouldn't. But now that we know the way . . . It's quite distressing, don't you know, how quickly familiarity sets in. A helicopter to the office; sheeps' eyes on toast; the second look into Chapman's Homer . . '

'But would it work? Again?' asked Rimmer.

'You mean is it still there or can we attain to it? When you visit as many queer places as I do . . '

'What is your line exactly?'

'You might describe me, I suppose, as an itinerant. But when it's Lesotho today, Rwanda tomorrow and not even Lesotho and Rwanda but a particular field of weeds half way up a hillside in the Hololo valley and a swamp full of cane and crocodiles twenty-five kilometres outside Kigali . . . the very preciseness of the locations, if you follow me, gives them the appearance of stage settings erected for my benefit. Are they still there when I'm back in the Holiday Inn?'

'Always the Holiday Inn. A stage setting in itself. In Maseru some time ago they were showing the same pornographic film I had seen in Amsterdam years before, only with the reels in the wrong order. Not that it made much difference, even to the climax, if you will pardon the expression. But it was both marginally stimulating and oddly comforting, rather like that pub. The observed ritual of copulation is not unlike that of the solitary drinkers—did you notice them? Lift, pause, sip, lower, lift, pause, sip . . . Improperly dressed as I was I felt more at home than I'm sure I will do when I land officially in Dublin . . . When was it you said you had left?'

'Yesterday,' said A N Other, 'if the word has any meaning. My watch is going again. But that's natural enough at our age: life through the wrong end of the telescope, sex safely in the head.'

'Speak for yourself. This time I'll go first.' He moved to get up.

'Hold hard,' said A N Other, 'would you look at the cut of your man over there.'

Rimmer followed his gaze, which was fixed on a middle-sized, wizened individual sweating profusely in a heavy tweed jacket and looking around him with all the appearance of extreme dislocation.

'I see him. One of ours. Must have found his way in here after half a dozen circuits—how long are we grounded?—looking for the bar.'

'Supposing,' said A N Other, 'that he's come the other way.'

'My way? Hardly likely. The clothes, for one thing. You wouldn't get yourself up in that garb leaving Maseru or wherever, even if bound for clammier climes.'

'That's not what I mean. He could have come through the door. Forwards rather than backwards.'

'In which case he has my sympathy,' said Rimmer, 'the price of drink, for one thing.' The man looked over to them, eyes clearing as he registered A N Other's brogue. 'Be careful. He's recognised you for what you are and whence you came. He'll be over to us in a minute to prove beyond reasonable doubt that you both share the same seventeenth cousin.' But the man sank back against the pale sepia wall of the restaurant as if into an old photograph, the unidentifiable stranger caught behind the smiling family group on O'Connell Bridge.

'We had better make some kind of hole in this,' Rimmer added, raising his glass. 'O dear.' He peered shortsightedly at the bottle. 'Tanzanian rosé. I wonder why they bother.'

'I first met up with it in a rather nice open-air restaurant on the road down to Dar,' said A N Other. 'They were so pleased we had ordered it that we hadn't the heart to leave a drop, though it was nearly the finish of us.'

'At least it's an attempt, I suppose. There's an Irish white wine too—or there was, last time I was home. Tastes like diluted embalming fluid.'

'No body?'

'Give me five,' said Rimmer, 'and knock. Like this.'

5

As nonchalantly as possible, though the normal mode of entering a gents' toilet at that point eluded him, he went in, closing the door behind him but—taking a chance—omitting to swing over the gnawed chrome handle to secure the ostensible privacy. Instead of the conventional layout, door facing onto bowl, cistern and other accoutre ...

A N Other had scarcely given him two. '*Emicat in terris non Vallis amoenior illa*,' he intoned, performing the door-closing ceremony with scarcely a glance at his surroundings: '*Obvia qua miscent flumina bina sinus.*'

'I'm sorry,' said Rimmer, 'I never took Latin further than Littlego. Barely even that. *By this name she veils her crime, sitting stratisque relictis* ... What was it anyway?'

'A poor thing but mine own. Well, almost. Fragment of a College exercise. Come now: *emicat in terris non Vallis* ...'

'Reverberations chapter seventeen?'

'Hardly, though I bow to your scriptural knowledge. Our fellow-alumnus Tom Moore. The Meeting of the Waters. An old joke, but I thought appropriate in the circumstances. *Spiritus ante meus tenues vanescet in auras* ... but the rest won't come to me.'

'*As the vale in whose bosom the sweet waters meet,*' sang Rimmer, experimentally and untunefully. 'No, nor me—in English or anything else. Have you ever seen Shakespeare in Kiswahili? *Omlette, omlette, ninakuwa papaspooki* ...'

'Remember there is, or was, no singing,' said A N Other. 'No television, no radio with bright commercial voices prophesying dandruff, no pub grub except the curly hang sangwich, no women. What in heavens name did we see in them?'

'The pints. And we can't even be sure they'll still be there. It was closing time, all the bonafides with fictitious addresses outside the three-mile limit well on their way. Found acting suspiciously on licensed premises after permitted hours. Defendants, who claimed to have travelled the statutory distance, could produce no credible proof of identity. Their manner of dress suggested . . .'

'And that's another thing. We'll have to find something more appropriate to the age and station.'

'A curate's apron?' suggested Rimmer. 'It would cover a multitude.'

It was a heavy footfall, of the kind made by army boots. Their voices, raised in expectation, must have been clearly audible. At the bottom of the door the ten centimetre gap confirmed the impression, only there was more the suggestion of police—military police perhaps. There's three of them in gaol now, he had overheard at the party in Lusaka, caught with two passports. We are allowed to take in food, but there's little doubt that they are being regularly beaten. The next morning at the roadblock by the bridge, the circle of nervous young men with guns. The boot was joined by another, followed by the blow of a fist on the door. It could have been the waiter/cashier, standard issue boots, come to tell them that their rosé was getting warm . . .

A N Other jerked an urgent thumb in the direction of the second door. It opened, as neither had observed the last time, as if off its hinges. A second loud blow followed them into . . .

'The trouble is,' said Rimmer, 'that once you've seen one you've seen them all. Concentrating on the basic function, how much of the decor do you take in? Unless, of course, you're here for a more serious purpose, sitting stratisque relictis looking for something to read.'

'Precisely,' said A N Other, 'over there.'

Rimmer turned to the wall behind him, forgetting to put on his glasses. 'What's this?' He read out slowly, in a passable accent: *Un seui hêtre me manque et tout est des peupliers.*

'Not one of my languages,' said A N Other, 'more's the pity. I had, of course, the best of intentions—always have had, with every new posting. But somehow they never got beyond the accidentally-memories teach-yourself phrases. I used to know the Kibuji for *Look at grandmother's neck* and used it on every possible occasion.'

'There's another,' said Rimmer. The light was dim, the inscription either faded or badly written in what looked like old-fashioned bottle ink. 'Some kind of poem,' he hazarded, 'at least in English this time, I think.' He read out, sotto voce, mindful of the boot under the door:

> *The Hired Man*
> *Today I saw down her tree.*
> *Tomorrow I saw up her tree.*
> *Yesterday I saw up her skirt.*

'What kind of carry-on is that? A bit too clever by half.'

'Precisely,' said A N Other, re-embracing the word. 'Take the two together.' He too spoke in an undertone, but no sound reached them other than the gentle pullulation of a distant splarge. 'Put them together and what do you deduce?'

'Some person or persons exhibiting a juvenile wit.'

'Not bad, Rimmer. And where might you expect to encounter such persons? *Laudamus te benignissime Pater pro serenissimis Regina Elizabetha . . .'*

'You think so? It would certainly explain the graffiti including (he had his glasses on now) that representation of what I take to be an expectant pudendum. Though it might indeed be an academic eye seeking an absconded pupil.' He looked round him. The cubicle was, apart from the eclectic graffiti, unremarkable. The apartment in which it was installed appeared, however, to have been built on generous proportions, with a lofty ceiling. From somewhere came the tinkling of a badly-tempered piano: somebody was murdering the Brahms Rhapsody number 2 in G minor, opus 79.

'The music. Yes. I used to try to play that myself, hour after hour on the College . . .'

'Where?'

'Where else but number 4. Was it 4? In the corner of Front Square, next to . . .'

'The jacks. I think you have hit it.'

'Why else but that we have in some way brought it upon ourselves. What were we talking about before that knock came to the door—the other door?'

'Yes, of course. The meeting of the waters. One of those things that transports you back in . . .'

'And I can go on now: *Quam corde immemori concidet iste locus . . .'*

'Please don't. Other—I'll take your word for it. But when, though? Am I to be even more conspicuous in my cutty sark, fallen among Edwardian fops?'

'I was back here—this is if this is here—sometime in the '60s,' said A N Other. 'It must have been after an interval of nearly five years, mostly in—well, never mind where, I walked through Front Gate (I'm not Dublin, don't you know, and had little occasion to be in the city) as much to pass half an hour between appointments as anything else. Certainly not a sentimental journey. Summer, probably, at the start of the long vacation. I remembered our working for Mod., sitting in the long, warm evenings on the steps of the Dining Hall after Commons, being photographed by intrusive Americans in our gowns.'

'Americans in your gowns?'

'I used to remember our indignation when called upon in subsequent years to point a camera at unimpressed Kibuji warriors in the cause of duty. But then I walked on into New Square. Almost deserted except for two people sitting on the grass, playing chess, watched by a third. Nothing in that, except that all three were stripped to the waist. And when black, I think it was, moved knight to king's bishop three (I prefer the old notation) and turned to the observer for approval I saw it was a girl. Pure Monet, or Minet or Manet. I was never sure.'

'In our day she would have been fined five shillings for sitting on the grass. *G F Mitchell, Junior Dean, chanced to come upon the scene* . . . as someone wrote in the *Miscellany* of altogether another misdemeanour.'

'You see, Rimmer? Would you have recalled that fragment of doggerel without the imperative of the *genus loci*?'

'You may be right. All we can do is go and see.' He made a move towards the door.

'If I might suggest,' said A N Other, 'I am the more properly dressed, given that we are correct in our temporal assumptions.'

'Suppose we are but it's high summer? The suit, if you will forgive me . . .'

'I shall behave erratically, mutter to myself, shower intemperate greetings on teetotal strangers, stagger impulsively in my walk, trespass on pedicured lawns. A sure method of escaping detailed observation. The Kibuji employ it, if detected in some embarrassing action such as polishing another woman's cooking pot, for creating an instant and face-saving persona. You know, Rimmer, I am feeling a good deal better. It could be put down either to a remission of the Tanzanian rosé or the unsullied air of the fifties—for it is there, I hazard, we shall find ourselves. I shall leave you. On no account venture forth—particularly, I would suggest, should that piano-playing cease. Four knocks.'

'*Where?*' asked Rimmer, confused by the memory of a long-forgotten name on a map.

The cubicle door, opening and shutting, had afforded him a glimpse of a general ground plan which would have been sufficient to confirm A N Other's theory had not the unseen pianist, struggling now with the repeat of the first section of the Brahms, offered him an even less assailable, if disquietingly equivocal, affirmation. If the music itself was timeless (he had himself forced the clouding memory of the *mezza voce* triplets out of arthritic fingers onto deliquescent keyboards in decaying residences of former colonial masters in several African countries) the manner of its execution (and the verb, he felt, was not misplaced) was oppressively familiar, occasioning him an embarrassment he could not account for. He felt himself stiffen—at his age!—as the unseen fingers of the left hand fumbled the dotted quaver octaves of the bass, found himself anticipating with certainty the badly broken chord from the centre of which an inexcusable E flat would inevitably emerge like a slug from under a stone. Suddenly, in the middle of the cross-hands section in which the pianist, as he knew he would, failed to come within a mile of the top F, the music stopped, an echoing silence followed by the slam of the piano lid and the rustle (the capacitating elements of which he could discern as clearly as if he were seeing it) of tattered scores roughly settling together. A chair scraped, footsteps, and the heavy oak door was being opened. An intense compulsion to catch even a glimpse of the poor musician seized him even as something equally unaccountable held him back. Before he had resolved the dilemma the footsteps had faded. Lowering a cracked, paintless wooden seat (we are at least, he thought, in a pre-plastic age) he sat down to wait.

6

A N Other was scanning a large poster pinned up underneath the notice-boards. *DO YOU WANT TO BE A CHARMER?* it enquired in crudely executed lettering: *DO YOU WANT TO BE A QUEEN? AND YOU SIR—A SEWAGE FARMER? . . .*

'One of the English contingent who couldn't get into Sheffield,' offered Rimmer, 'there were no sewage farms in Ireland in 1950.'

'*THE MOD. LANG. DANCE,*' read A N Other, skipping to the bottom line. 'Can you imagine?'

He found he could imagine all too well. The path to the Dixon Hall through College Park lit up on Saturday night for the protection of the innocent. The Great White Way. Crumbling conversation in the last dance under the bored eyes of the chaperones; too unsure to offer to bike out with her on her High Nellie to Virginity Hall. Or the Metropole Ballroom, uncle Bob's dress trousers, some fabric like sandpaper lining the crotch. Gin and orange and the taste of sexual defeat, never drunk it since. Spot prize. First gentleman up here with a pair of ladies' . . . all the near-schoolboys had assumed gloves, rushed up before the words were out. Only a few canny ex-servicemen, with the kind of partners only available to the ex-servicemen, had hung back, reading the MC's mind. Just one girl, however, consented, and they were black. He'd dreamt about them.

While A N Other continued to scan the notices covering the entire hexagon—or was it octagon?—of Front Gate, Rimmer stood looking out across the square. In front of the Campanile a brand-new Morris Minor had attracted an interested group. Two girls were picking their way in high heels and long skirts precariously across the cobbles, watched by two young men in subfusc sports jackets in the doorway of number 7. One of the girls, tall, blonde and willowy, succeeded in holding her head in something close to a posture of splendid disdain which very nearly concealed the fact that every two or three steps she was obliged to look down at her feet like an unrehearsed piano-player (the simile cost him some effort) while the other, short and dumpy, the black fringe contributing to the air of a standoffish Cairn terrier, had a face so fixed in her time that he was almost certain he remembered her—though the image he had carried forward into the future, on the rare occasions he had thought of her at all, was not one of this rather lost-looking little girl but of someone more poisedly elegant and, he now realised, a good deal more sexy. She glanced up at him as she passed, her features disappointingly registering no trace either of interest or recognition. But then he was, now, old enough to be (resisting the thought as if its connotations were incestuous) her great-uncle. Defendant, your honour, stated that he was only endeavouring to refamiliarise himself with certain obsolescent mechanisms—his words, your honour. I think he was referring to ladies, er, suspenders. That will do, thank you, sergeant. I will not have this court turned into a sodom and begorr . . .

'Rimmer! Would you look at this.'

A N Other had adapted himself so amiably to the circumambience of the gown that he suspected him of concealing, or rather failing to admit, a continuing academic function. Only the one, he had explained, after the four knocks: 'I had to use all my charm and a fake Australian accent—not too broad, of course—to coax a loan of it from the Porters' Lodge. Promised I would have it back within the hour, whatever that might mean in this context.'

'But why the gown?'

'The perfect disguise for you, of course. Nearly nude you may be by 1950s standards—and that would seem to be where we find ourselves—but academically nude you shall not be.'

But the gown, when Rimmer tried it on in the confines of the cubicle, had reached nearly to the ankles.

'Never mind,' said A N Other, undismayed, 'I will wear it and in the eye of the beholder it will connote us both. I shall masquerade as a member of one of the obscurer faculties.'

'In a *Scholar's* gown?' Rimmer was pleased at having recollected the essential difference.

A N Other was unmoved. 'I'll carry it off, since I will only be occupying a secondary role. You, Rimmer, are the visiting academic from wherever on the way to give a visiting lecture on whatever. What do you know about that isn't too locked into the future? Something you stopped learning about after you left College? Fix your mind, if you can, on what hasn't happened. Are you any good at archaeology?'

'Newgrange? Fourknocks? But I'd be lost if I meet somebody, say, with Linear B in his bonnet. I'd be happier with something more offbeat—maybe American. In College they were still a race apart, if you recall: their clothes, the accents, above all their childlike naïveté. Though I admit I was wrong about both rock-and-roll and jeans. Never thought either would last jig-time.'

'And rain checks.'

'Rain checks. And those funny words like *uh-huh* in American novels. I never found out what they meant and then it was too late to ask.'

'And I always hoped I would find a cancelled rain check lying around in some American hotel. Pay the deserts of Wad Medani . . . How about D. Mort. S.?'

'Come again?'

'Doctor of Mortuary Science,' explained A N Other. 'I met one once, years ago. He seemed quite proud of it.'

'But I know nothing of mortuary science,' Rimmer protested.

'Nor will anyone else we are likely to meet. Can you imagine the polite enquiry of the Regius Professor of Divinity, whoever he was—is. I'll remember in a minute.'

'You won't. I've tried to put names on three or four people I thought I should remember. There's some kind of blockage.'

'But would you ever look at this?' A N Other was examining another poster. *'BIENNIAL INTERUNIVERSITY DEBATE. THAT THE PAST IS NO PASSPORT TO THE PRESENT. MR REES-MOGG OF THE OXFORD UNION. MR ST. JOHN STEVAS OF THE CAMBRIDGE UNION.* Names mean anything to you?'

'No,' said Rimmer, 'I was never in the Hist.'

'Now is your chance to repair the omission.'

'But we can't. I mean if we weren't there in the first place. There must be accurate attendance records, unforgiving minutes.'

'Indubitably. But have you observed that the date, according to a calendar I took a quick look at in the Porters' Lodge, is almost certainly Wednesday the eighth of March 1950. But the evening (I take it to be evening by the angle of the sun and the girls scurrying to leave the precincts before six) suggests the summer. Time is, for no clear reason, out of joint. I hazard a guess that we will leave no lasting impression.'

'You mean people will see through us, like Mr O?'

'Not if we are circumspect. Are you absolutely sure you weren't at that debate?'

'Absolutely. I always loathed formal debates and that class of thing. Ironic that I seem to have spent most of my life attending meetings. But why the concern?'

A N Other did not answer, though Rimmer barely registered the lacuna. He was staring fixedly at a girl, managing better than most, crossing the cobbles towards them. It was indeed she. Yesterday I saw up her skirt. Though it had been the other's in fact, out in the flat in Ballsbridge. Lying flat on the floor after a fruitless attempt to persuade her to tell him where she had got the drugs, she standing over him—whether accidentally or on purpose he was too young to tell—the French leg offering him his first prospect of the unpromised land. Whereas this was the one he had wanted, or thought he had wanted. *Darling, what I say is true, any place on earth will do just so long as I have you . . .* attempting to show him, in an unregarded corner of the Dixon, the steps of the foxtrot he would never master. *My happiness.* Oh. The girl, her attention held by the poster for LE HOT CLUB DE DUBLIN at Cafolla's Broadway Café, turned suddenly as if his finger had run down her spine, eyes wary with half-recognition. Should he? Speak?

But the gap, all of three metres, seemed unbridgeable. She had always kept her distance, even, somehow, in those inconclusive encounters in the sagging armchair, his wife tactfully away practising dropkicks in the Park. Virtually everything, he had soon discovered, was out of play—to his untutored touch at least. And that was how she had described, on the one occasion she had consented to come and listen, his playing of . . .

'Have we enough left for a drink?' A N Other was following his gaze without any apparent curiosity, 'if we can trust the clock we have about an hour before the Hist. meeting. Mooney's in College Green? A bottle of their burgundy and a sandwich?'

Rimmer, groping in his trousers pocket, saw the girl still half-looking at him, her feet angled uncertainly. Second class Mod. in French and German. Her telling him how, when she wore that funny furry coat into the freezing lecture room in Number Thirty-five, Dr Scheyer had said 'Ah, Miss Cameron, I see you in your pelt.' And instead of laughing, he had twitched with the embarrassment of believing that she was believing that he was mentally undressing her. The confusion he felt now was just as real as his eyes went out on stalks apparently of their own volition and positioned themselves down between her . . .

'Ten, twelve and six,' he counted, clumsy with the old money, 'fifteen shillings give or take. We could go and see what would it get us. I haven't eaten since . . .'

'Or we could go back,' said A N Other, as the girl turned, glanced briefly at the board to see had anyone left her an invitation to coffee in Robt. Roberts', made her way through Front Gate.

'Go back?'

'Another drop of the Tanzanian, a goat sandwich on the house. The flights might even be called. Where would that leave us?'

But before Rimmer could consider the question, a voice—Corkonian in its undulations—broke in upon them, the resonance winging round the octagon or hexagon like a well-oiled bat. 'Of course to the student of political science the Irish sovereign legislature and flexible constitution of 1782 are cause for just pride. The appointment of judges, as you will no doubt recall, was vested in the Lord Chancellor of Ireland, and never perhaps was a more independent bench known. The noble action of Kilwarden, C J in Wolfe Tone's case . . .'

The Pope O'Mahony, talking his way into an early entrance at the Hist., paused in mid-sentence whilst taking in the two apparently senior figures. Recognition flickered, began to glow behind the thick glasses as the mental card-index was riffed for a name to put to a face. His companion, a deferential young man, waited patiently for further news of Wolfe Tone. Rimmer, frozen with indecision, made no move, offered not so much as a nod. The Pope's assorted garments, the unmakings of several ensembles, were the same that he seemed to remember from some years later—that is, some years earlier. Recognition of some kind could scarcely be avoided.

Pretending avid interest in his watch, still stopped, he took A N Other by the arm, steering him through what was now a steady dribble of people coming into College, motioning him to shed the gown as he did so. The voice, resuming in a high register, but with now something of a mechanical ring to it, as if its owner were still searching the file, followed them: '. . . stands out as an example. In '98 when Tone was captured and sentenced to be hanged, John Philpot Curran made an application to the King's Bench for a writ of habeas cor . . .'

'A close-run thing.' Rimmer's voice was unsteady with relief. 'He would have known me for sure—I couldn't have been less than thirty when we met for the last time. A man doesn't change that much. Or does he?'

'And supposing he had?'

'What could I have told him? That this man's son is my son's father? That I once gave him the granny's maiden name and he had my lineage worked back to devious roots before I had the tea poured?'

'I never knew him,' said A N Other, 'but then I never really knew anybody. Looking back on it . . .'

But Rimmer, as they walked out the gate and turned right towards Tom Moore, was a stranger in a strange land. No Pope here. Had he expected his own snail-trails, the dried slime of forty years, to be visible on the pitted surface of College Green? There were only the tramlines, curving their way round into Nassau Street, dulled with disuse. As he watched one of the new, shiny green number 8 buses which had (if their agreed estimate was right) only recently supplanted the last of the line, the expected pang of nostalgia failed to materialise. Too many years, too many termini: buses in Bangkok, trams in Hong Kong, erosion in Hololo, hunger in Jarso: what, in these converging contexts, was an abandoned tramtrack? As they turned the corner in College Street he noted with the kind of puzzled recognition one extends to an unfaded family photograph the die-stamper's shop, the as yet unamalgamated bank and the fusty façade of Mooney's. The often recurring nightmare: stepping onto the stage in a role yet to be written.

'And of course,' he said to A N Other, when they were installed at the bar, the bottle of burgundy and two hang sangwidges between them, 'we are not really here. I mean we can't be.'

'I refute you thus,' retorted Other, taking an appreciative sip from his glass, 'never could afford this in College days, even if I had acquired the taste. But on various visits back . . .'

Rimmer was not to be put off. 'My point exactly. If we were really here we would have been here, if you follow me. Or, to put it another way, we would be here now. We would be sitting here, in this exact place . . .'

'But we are sitting here, in this exact place.'

'No, with respect. If we had been sitting here—are sitting here—on Wednesday March the whatever 1950 we would be sitting here in the appropriate, how shall I put it, corporeal envelope . . .'

'And we, in our present age and station, would be of the genus doppleganger, is that it?'

Rimmer looked at him as he had not, he realised, looked at him before. Tall—about six feet nothing; greying hair still relatively abundant; eyes, as he focused contentedly on his drink, that did not demand glasses; spare frame with little evidence of indulgence; sober Magee suit that, even with its executive cut . . .

'Were there—are there—executives in 1950?'

'It was not a word to conjure with.'

'But there's no way . . .'

'Don't employ that appalling locution. It will betray us immediately for what we are not.'

'Point taken. But what did we say instead? Have you ever noticed how the cliché utterly obliterates what it subsumes, so that you cannot remember what came before the moment in time when . . .'

'Most of them sound as if they had fallen out of one of the Evensong collects: *Almighty and most merciful Father, who hast safely taught us, at the end of the day* . . .'

'You haven't answered my question. Since we are both here in the corporeal shape of another era and since we both admit not to have patronised this particular establishment—to the extent, at least, of drinking its burgundy—in 1950 or thereabouts, it follows that our presence here must be so immaterial as to be undetectable.'

'The barman took the money,' observed A N Other mildly.

'Except for the King Mosheshoe item I had to pull back in a hurry. Lesotho was—is—still in the Empire. Under some other name.'

'And remains so, except that it's the tricolour that's flying over the Post Office. Ever spent a long summer evening with ex-pat wives? The *Irish Times* the other day (I speak of the future) spelt it e-x-p-a-t-r-i-o-t when writing of an ex-colleague. Surely grounds for libel. But it wrote truer than it knew. You can't blame them. Stuck in a home away from home while the husbands are out all day remaking the Third World in our image. No distractions but . . .'

'Hang gliding?' Rimmer, with a flick of the wrist, sent his sangwidge skidding along the counter.

'To travel is, hopefully, better than to arrive,' said A N Other, retrieving the curly sliced pan from a proximate puddle of stout, 'serves you right if you get smoked salmonella.'

'And expire before my time? Now that . . .'

'Good evening, gentlemen. I think I have had the pleasure. It would be about a year ago—correct me if I'm wrong.'

The shaking hand was holding a badly-folded copy of the *Evening Mail*. Mandrake gestured hypnotically. Rimmer was fingering the few coins left in his pocket.

'A small one, Mr O?'

He stole a glance as he ordered. The same reach-me-down suit, or its close relation. The shakes no better and no worse. But he nevertheless felt he was looking back at him over an elapsed twelve months, observing a slight lateral dislocation as if he had shuffled a couple of steps sideways towards his quietus. And given their ages (for on this plane they must be near-contemporaries) had he, Mr O, quietly observed a similar phenomenon? In friends encountered after thirty, twenty, even ten years, he had become used to reading the signs and ignoring them, ah, sure you're good for another thirty years yet, as if that would somehow underwrite a similar insurance on himself. He shuddered, the sharp spasm nearly overturning the Power he was placing in front of Mr O, whose vagrant forefinger, orientated towards some private magnetic north, was making a spasmodic effort to stab at a blurred newspaper picture (Rimmer had again discarded the glasses) somewhere off the periphery of Mandrake. It looked as much as anything like a set of pigeonholes on wheels, perhaps some unremembered child's toy.

'Way off the mark,' said Mr O, 'it's one of those things, in a manner of speaking, that transports you back in time. Second battle of Noeux-les-Mines.' He rhymed it with vines.

'The last post,' suggested Rimmer, grasping at fugitive recollections of railway sorting coaches beached in sidings in Amiens Street.

'Motor pigeon-cotes was the name they put on them. Though they were nothing, if the truth were told, other than a double-decker bus with the top taken off and a pigeon loft put in its place. The very same. Now' (the finger stabbed again) 'I see where they're after discovering one on some old battlefield—some battle the Dubs. had a hand in anyway. And the powers that be are going to present it to this new transport museum where they're going to put the trams as came off the Dalkey line. I served me time on the Sandymount route—that's why they gave me the job. You remember the little single-deckers were built specially to get under the railway bridge? Ah, no' (he paused to peer at Rimmer with almost malignant curiosity) 'perhaps that was before your time. And the first war itself?'

'Too old for the first, too young for the second, I'm afraid. But their use must have been very limited, surely? Apart from being, as you might say, a sitting duck of a target?'

'Well you might,' agreed Mr O, 'most of the stuff tied to the legs of those lads was from the top brass—those few of them that ever ventured as far as the front line—to their lady-loves back at base. Oh I know what you're thinking—that we made a few little substitutions here and there. But true bill, those Frog pigeons didn't know half the time whether they were coming or going—footless on foraged barley. We used take a look at what came back, of course, on the QT. Most of it was in Frog language, but there was the odd one that even got past old Mickey Joe, who could parlez-vous as well as the next man. Answers to questions that had never been asked. One I remember to this day because it was in Irish. Would you credit it?'

He paused for a ruminative sip.

'I'd been one of the early Gaeilgeoirí when as the man says it was neither popular nor profitable and I had enough still to put English on it: *BÁS CRUA LEIS NA CÓINÍNÍ*—old rabbits die hard, as you might say. We, that's myself and the co-driver, man by the name of Ber Bodkin from Denmark Street, thought it meant that our numbers were up. You were the lucky one, being too old. There was no stopping me, the rights of small nations and all that carry-on. Where was I in 1916? Driving that bloody bird-cage in and out of every shellhole in Flanders. You'd miss the trams, but . . .'

I used to, regularly, thought Rimmer. Letting myself out of the flat, leaving her in what I thought was some kind of trance, before I knew better. Lightly rummaged but no more: because she seemed so indifferent to my modest advances they stopped in their tracks. Like the one I ran for to the kiosk at the bottom of Pembroke Road: sorry son, the power's gone, you'd be as quick to walk. And having to knock for the porter at nearly one in the morning and being reported to the JD. The lure of monasticism— or the nearest any diffident Irish protestant could allow himself to come to it: cocoa (cocoa!) round a winter fire, self-deprecating games of Up-the-Auntie, all the argued complexities reducing themselves, by three in the morning, to the singular enigma *What is your definition of happiness?* The homely domestic noises: someone pouring a bottle of stout through your letterbox after a Hist. blind. Someone else chopping up a sofa out in the bleak fast-nesses of Botany Bay . . .

'Let's go,' he said, 'or we'll never make that meeting.'

A N Other, who, taking advantage of his position on Rimmer's far side, had avoided any direct conversation with Mr O, looked relieved.

'You'll have one for the road,' said the latter, with little conviction.

'Another time,' said Rimmer. 'We'll get you again.' Wondering whether the phrase had any contemporary currency. But Mr O, apparently having already dismissed them from his consciousness, was shakily revamping his *Mail*.

'When does it arrive? The pigeon-carrier?' asked Rimmer, blundering into politeness.

There was no answer. Mr O's attention was apparently absorbed by an underwear advertisement from which all exposed portions of the female figure had been modestly excised. *CAMI-KNICKERS 50 PERCENT OFF* he read out: 'That class of thing should be reported to the Censorship Board. Why in the name of Jaysus couldn't they say fifty percent on? It's the same difference and would cause no offence. It's on the way, by all reports, across England, though if it's under its own steam it'll be a bloody miracle. Those Frog engines were the very divil, though, fair dues, get them started and they'd run for ever. They'll never get it onto the *Princess Maud,* but. Have to bring her in through the North Wall or Rosslare. Fifty percent off. Spirella and her wonderful corset— sure the country is going to the dogs. Here, don't be leaving your coat. You'll freeze out there in that tennis get-up.'

Rimmer picked up the gown and followed A N Other out of the bar. 'I need to go to the jacks,' he said as the night air hit them. March air?

'So do I. But I think we had better go back the way we came.'

'You mean back to . . .'

'Yes.' A N Other was patently uneasy. 'Something's wrong. The weather's changed. We're only half in it. Things could get out of hand very easily. Did you notice the wine?'

'It wasn't as I remembered it. But then things never are.'

'It was the Tanzanian, whatever about the label.'

'You're sure? And Mr O? Mind you, I think he can see through us. Avoided asking any questions. Seemed relieved that however much of us was there wasn't staying.'

It came towards them in a gentle glide as they stood waiting to cross the road by Tom Moore, a number 15 tram of the open-ended or balcony type, its bell clanging, trolley hissing gently on the wire.

'Worse than I thought,' said A N Other. 'The 15s went off about 1948. And the cars look decidedly older.'

'Auto-suggestion? We were talking, if you remember, about trams. That gown will never find its way back again. But then I have the theory that every time I misplace my glasses, about seventeen times a day, they disappear irresponsibly into another era.'

'Making spectacles of themselves in an eighteenth-century drawing room? Unlikely, come on, *ad monti nostri*. Let us hope that the somewhat fetid air of number 4 is still full of eastern promise.'

The airside door was still closed, apparently as they had left it. They let themselves out cautiously, one by one, A N Other first. By the time Rimmer had caught up with him he was seated at their table, for all as if he had never left it. The Tanzanian rosé, half-drunk, was still in place, the scattering of other passengers and the waiter/cashier acknowledging nothing untoward.

'I think I see how it works,' said A N Other, 'you are partially right about the auto-suggestion. The fact that the image of this place was foremost in our minds probably guaranteed our safe return.'

'You mean if I had suddenly started thinking about the Holiday Inn . . . ?'

'Possibly.'

'And the trams?'

'*Mea culpa*. While Mr O was engaging in that tedious monologue my ideas were developing along other lines.'

'But so were mine. I suppose under the circumstances we can consider ourselves lucky we didn't end up at the second battle of wherever-it-was, covered in pigeon-shit. Nevertheless . . .'

The waiter/cashier was beside them, proffering a menu.

'No thank you,' said Rimmer, 'we've seen it.'

'You take,' insisted the waiter, 'different.'

Rimmer took. *DINER FOR DELAYING PASSENGERS. OMIT 2 TO RESTAURANT, SOAP OF THE DAYS, FARACED PIGGIN A LA FRANCES.*

'Which means,' said A N Other, 'that the delay is infinitely extensible. ATC strike, perhaps. Or the Third World at war.'

'We could try the piggin. Or, on the other hand, we could go back. Think of a date and stick to it. Follow procedures. It would be nice to get it right.'

'They've reprinted Djuna Barnes,' said A N Other. 'I bought a paperback for the journey. Pity it's on the plane. I'd forgotten it, but it was all the rage where we're going—if we're going. The *in* book, don't you know, even in the sacred precincts of Classics. They—somebody, the Mod. Lang., the English Group, the Chuff-Chuff Club—even hung a debate on it. *That this house agrees that the Irish are impatient for eternity.* I think it was one of the rare occasions on which I spoke. No one, of course, in those days, had ever sat in an airport for twenty-four hours.'

'Never heard of him,' said Rimmer.

'Her.'

'Her. My literary tastes were very ordinary, if I remember. Stuff left over from school. *Myself when young did eagerly frequent . . .* How's this it goes on?'

'It's not how it goes on,' said A N Other with some show of excitement, 'but how it finishes. De da de da de da *but evermore came out by the same door as in I went.* And how did I remember that?'

'As an omen,' said Rimmer, managing to swallow a mouthful of the rosé, 'I would say it is a good deal better than the entrails of a farced bird. We will proceed with both circumspection and concentration. It tastes like Mooney's burgundy. And I would rather like to see my wife.'

7

'Marx,' the man with the forelock was saying.

'Harpo's bizarre,' affirmed the girl with glasses, magazine under her arm. They walked off hand-in-hand towards the Reading Room.

It had been an easy passage back. The gown, for some reason, was still where they had discarded it, down beside the bowl; they had decided against trying to return it to the Porters' Lodge on discovering they had lost their year. Someone, however, had removed the pile of torn-up newspaper and substituted a largely unused roll of Bronco.

'Prosperity,' said A N Other: 'I hope we haven't made a bags of it again. That has all the look of the '60s.'

But when they emerged, again cautiously, again one by one (A N Other first on account of the suit) they were reasonably sure they were on time. They had projected the year 1950 as being one they both vaguely remembered, for different reasons; and because they had already had some little re-experience of it. They had also opted for Trinity Term, refraining only from naming the day since neither had to hand a 1950 calendar. Whilst pretending to pee in the airside jacks, waiting for a rumpled passenger to depart, they had discussed money. Rimmer's pound was reduced to sevenpence halfpenny. It was A N Other who recalled he had had a modest bank account in the Hibernian, College Green, during his College career. The only problem was getting at it. Simple, Rimmer had suggested: go in, ask for a cheque, explaining that you have forgotten your cheque book. But they knew me—know me, A N Other had objected, as a merry young man of twenty. To which Rimmer had replied that the trick would be to ask for a cheque without identifying himself.

'Bring it out and make it out to me. Sign it and I will go in and collect.'

'But what about identification. You can't very well show them a credit card. A passport would arouse suspicion, even if you kept your thumb over the date. Nobody went anywhere in 1950.'

'You aren't remembering,' said Rimmer. 'We were an innocent generation. Cars left unlocked in Dawson Street, bicycles propped against lamp-posts, the key in the door. They probably won't ask for anything.'

'That tennis gear, as Mr O called it, won't do much for you. And ballpoint pens were only for the rich. I vaguely knew the son of the inventor in College. Big heavy things that filled your pockets with ink.'

'Only at high altitudes—like the top of the Rubrics. I'll take the cheque in, carry the gown and use my D. Mort. S. voice. Don't make it too small: that will really arouse their suspicions.'

'You are overlooking one thing,' said A N Other, 'and I am using your own argument against you. If I have funds in the account they don't amount to much—we were, after all, poor scholarship students. And if I draw on them when I didn't, don't you know . . . the wrong story careening down into history, as a former superior of mine was wont to characterise the outcome of any action the implications of which . . .'

'Point taken. But if we get our hands on the money why should we worry? The act itself is surely its own validation. Something else will have to be rearranged to accommodate it.'

'The knock-on effect could be serious. What if we were to shoot Dev. as he addresses the Philosophical Society? I seem to remember he was in opposition so it must have been around 1950.'

'Someone threw a bottle at the Bishop of Sodor and Man,' said Rimmer. 'It missed. But this time round . . .'

So engrossed had they become in the speculation that before they could retreat into the cubicle another seedy traveller had come in and they had had to re-address themselves to the chipped porcelain, trying to coax a few token drops from an exhausted source.

'We will have to stop micturating like this,' said A N Other, 'people will begin to talk. Come on now while the coast is clear.'

As they stood outside number 4 in the warm summer sunshine Rimmer began to experience a real identity with his surroundings and began to plan his day like an excited tourist.

'You know what I'd really like to do? Go on Commons. High Table, of course. Imagine the Chateau Yquem '32, the Cockburn '29 . . .'

'The bread-and-butter pudding. Third class deck of the mailboat after a rough crossing. No thank you. As a student I had a delicate stomach.'

But Rimmer was not to be deflated, 'I could try a little Brahms on that oversprung piano. The fingers might shed some of their arthritic spatulation. You know. Other, I feel forty years younger already.'

'I would caution you against that feeling. Remember that we're a couple of oul' fellas. Any attempt to discount that, particularly in one area, can only result in embarrassment and disaster. And I would also advise you against that piano. You might find it hard to explain yourself away—particularly to certain parties.'

'I am not sure that I follow you. But first things first. Money.'

The stratagem, rather to the surprise of both of them, worked. They agreed upon a sum of twenty pounds as being neither too large nor too small to cause comment and adequate to their needs—they were not, after all, proposing to linger. On A N Other's advice, Rimmer agreed to spend some of it—five guineas in Kevin & Howlin's and fifteen shillings in Switzer's, on a sports coat and shirt respectively, with a nondescript tie to complete the ensemble. He had reported that, on the whole, his American accent had worked reasonably well, though when he instructed the assistant to have a nice day the latter seemed a little uncertain as to how to proceed. Some interest was expressed, though of course, discreetly, in the fabric of his discarded shirt.

'I told them it was American too. I had forgotten, of course, how much greater was—is—our degree of cultural segregation. Americans are still people in loud clothes and cameras. Few of us have seen a Yank in the flesh, much less yearned to ape him.'

'Which is just as well for you,' said A N Other, 'the accent is wojous. At least I'm on safer ground with Australia. No one who went there ever came back.'

The brief expedition outside the walls had, nevertheless, not been without its alarms. Neither had said anything, but each had observed troubling inconsistencies. Tram wires were still strung along Nassau Street, though no tram appeared. It was the glimpse of something which, from a distance, bore the putative lineaments of a mobile pigeon-cote approaching from the direction of Robt. Roberts' café in Suffolk Street that had made them, by unspoken consent, retreat as rapidly as possible through Front Gate. The College was animatedly going about its business in a manner which made their assuming the casual occupancy of a lamp-post at the corner of Parliament Square a matter of no remark.

'Remember 1890,' said Other after a while, noting Rimmer's interest in the legs of a young lady, academically nude, hurrying in the direction of New Square.

'Not with you. You mean 1690, the pious, glorious and immortal memory? I was Northern on the grandfather's side, but they seem to have been for the most part that vanished breed, Protestant Home Rulers. It is hard, don't you think, and considering all that will happen, to realise that this is still the fortress of the Ascendancy, or what is left of it—barred to all right-thinking Catholics by archiepiscopal edict. I don't think then—now—I know a single Catholic. And you?'

'My wife is a Catholic,' said A N Other.

'That's strange,' said Rimmer, 'so was mine. But why 1890?'

'The year, give or take, you would have been born. That dates you. Forget those retreating calves; your place is in the chimney corner with the old woman of three cows. But *nil desperandum*. I suspect, from the general bustle and certain lack of academic decorum, that it is round or about Trinity Wednesday. I always wanted to gatecrash a party, but in those days I had neither the clothes nor the courage. Shall we investigate?'

Rimmer followed him in the direction of New Square, still recoiling from the abyss opened up by the prospect of 1890. 'One reason we are reasonably comfortable here,' he informed A N Other's back, 'is that we are within our lived experience. To be really cast adrift in the past, with no passport to the present . . .'

But, striding ahead on his long legs, Other wasn't listening. Rimmer wanted to ask him whether it was his intention that they should cling to their new personas, claiming to be their own uncles. How else could they approach the dead professors and senescent schoolboys, the baby-faced ex-servicemen with the stuck-on RAF moustaches, the young in one another's arms? He wanted to slit his crumpled corporeal envelope across the date-stamp, to step out, wise head on supple shoulders, and enjoy the worst of both worlds. But as he followed A N Other round the corner of the Rubrics, unskillfully dodging a bicycle, ten shillings for riding in a gown, the undifferentiated day grew harsh with long-focused reality. Trinity Wednesday 1950; having failed to be invited to any party and lacking, like A N Other, the courage to present himself unasked, he had proposed to Miss Cameron a small tête-à-tête in his rooms which, thanks to the College Races, would be otherwise untenanted. With the dregs of his term allowance he had bought half a bottle of Barsac from Morgan's and a cake from Bewley's. He had even, with more hope than conviction, put a vase or vawse of flowers in the bedroom. Plumping the cushions in the collapsing armchair, remembering at the last minute to extract a nail which had on the last occasion ruined a pair of nylons (his hope that she would discard them in his presence unrealised) he had, as the appointed hour of four approached, sat down to wait, the Junior Dean's postcard permission on the mantelpiece under the thatched cottage purloined from outside the Country Shop in Stephen's Green. He had waited. Four had struck. Then four-thirty. Then five. Outside the noise of merry-making was swelling. A raucous Northern voice was attempting 'The Sash . . .'

'A little early in the day,' said A N Other with distaste as the voice, from an upstairs window in number 33, began to choke on an excess of vomit, 'I think, politics apart, we would be wise to give that one a miss. The thing is to locate a party that will be suited to our age and station without allowing too much opportunity for those present to question our provenance, lively without putting too much strain on our . . .'

'How about RBD?' said Rimmer.

'I wish that sometimes you would let me finish a sentence,' said A N Other petulantly. 'RBD? Sounds like a new hallucinatory drug, but I know who you mean. I knew him slightly through Players.'

'It's worth a try. But he lived, as I remember, on the corner of the Bay. Back this way.'

They turned, but before they could retrace their steps a figure emerged from the doorway of number 33 clutching a champagne bottle.

'Good sh-sh-show! You must be the wife's people. Come on up. Wizard. Absolutely.'

They followed him up to the first floor, where the spillage from a set of rooms so tightly packed as to be virtually impenetrable had constituted itself a fringe party in its own right. Somebody pressed drink upon them and Rimmer found himself looking over the shoulder of a man clutching a copy of a student publication. He read the lines on the title page:

Remembering the pigeons on the grass,
Anxious to avoid the author's eye
I sit in the editorial office,
A clever mimic in a literary sty.

'That story, "Pigeons,"' the man was explaining to a plain, bored girl, 'was written by me.' He turned towards Rimmer, the by now familiar look of half-recognition on his face.

'Rimmer. Howard E Rimmer. On sabbatical from Milwaukee. Nice place you have here.'

'Henry Wilson,' the man responded in a lubricated Bally-mena accent, the look of puzzlement increasing. 'Haven't we met before?'

'I don't believe I've had the pleasure.' He was remembering Wilson, Mod. Lang. and something of a cricketer, someone with whom he had exchanged the odd remark on Commons, nothing more. 'You must meet my colleague . . .' But A N Other was visible only as a narrow back in a tight corner, and Wilson, the flicker of curiosity fading, was clearly more interested in trying to read the opening of his story to his unenthused companion. Scanning the faces, Rimmer was trying to put old heads on young shoulders, fixing on one glossy cranium which he recognised even before its owner turned to stare at him without any recognition and with the dismissive look of different generation. Yet he had drunk with this man, or with his balding, sixty-year-old surrogate, only months since in the Development Office in Dar-es-Salaam, relishing the air-conditioning after the sweaty drive down from Kilosa. They had agreed then that, though near contemporaries, they had never met in Trinity. But if he is here now I must, surely, have been here then, a fake American with a Birr? And over there in the rooms in the Rubrics, waiting for Miss Cameron . . . ?

'Hello. You look like a fish out of water.'

Rimmer remembered the name—Mullen—and the casual rudeness of the remark, word for word that with which he had greeted him when slithering, in Dar, out from behind a piece of greenery where he had been trying to tease a pet bush-baby. Here, however, he occupied the high ground, smugly confident that his disguise was impenetrable.

'I guess I am at that,' he replied, groping in his rag-bag of Americanisms for fragments of half-dissolved soap-operas and the detritus of pop lyrics. 'You-all live it up a bit too much for me, I reckon.'

'American?'

'I guess so. Elmer P Rimmer, Michigan. Here on sabbatical.'

'You don't look it, if you don't mind my saying so,' said Mullen. 'And, come to think of it, you don't sound it. No offence. You've lived abroad? I'm a colonial myself. And I think I've seen you somewhere before.'

'Could be,' said Rimmer, seeking a safe cliché, 'it's a small world.' Perhaps the man he had met in Dar was himself a blow-in, refugee from another era? Then the youthful face of Mullen suddenly fitted itself into a forgotten image of a Boat Club Regatta at Islandbridge, one of the few he had ever attended: an angry face emerging, a very wet dryad, from the Liffey into which he had been summarily deposited by Neptune—or some other unmannerly crew. Glimpsed only for a moment but apparently unconsciously recorded like—his memory now in free fall—a Bombay beggar, thrusting the stump of an arm through the window of a ricketty taxi; two shadowed figures, man and woman, in the entrance to a basement bar in Bratislava. Invitation to the vaults.

'Colonial, did you say? I guess I don't know a whole lot (that didn't sound right) about your British Empire. You a student here?' He remembered just in time to modify the vowel.

'Mental and Moral Science. *Bibo ergo sum.*' Mullen raised a glass, eyes cruising predatorily among the more localised women just as, in Dar, those of his latter-day self had gone widow-hopping (it was that kind of party) in the middle of a discussion, boring to both of them, of their common fund of unshared College memories.

'You must find it very different after . . . where did you say you came from?'

'I didn't. But it's Tanganyka, actually. Though of course I was sent off to school here. After some private tuition. The pater engaged a well-recommended Indian, but all I remember learning from him about Ireland was that Sir Walter Scott brought the carrot back from the New World and planted it in Youghal. Only he pronounced it "you-all"—like you Yanks.'

Rimmer laughed as he was expected to, the same laugh he had summoned when Mullen had told him the story, forty years later and a few months ago, over the diplomatic bag whiskey in Dar. He stopped himself just in time from responding with the anecdote, relating to a first secretary not yet born, with which he had countered on that occasion. Knowing the beginning and end of Mullen, the colonial insolence barely kept in check by a grace-and-favour job in Bilateral Aid, he saw with a sharp pang of recognition the beginning and end of himself, the pattern of anecdote more threadbare with each exposure, the very moderately successful young seducer on the poop deck on the voyage out—if you can't encompass it there you can't encompass it anywhere—reduced to . . . Though that young one over there now.

Mullen, intercepting the glance, frowned distaste. I don't like drinking outside my generation, his own son had told him when last they met, unconscious of the hurt. And his own father, pontificating into pints while he sipped dutifully, wondering when he could decently get away. Mullen double-shuffled, eyes like antennae.

'You'll excuse me. It was interesting to talk to you—' precisely as he had taken, or was to take, his dismissive leave in Dar, cutting a social swathe over to the unaccompanied grass widow of an engineer gone bush.

'Hello,' said a pale, decadent-looking young man, rather drunk, 'isn't this a repulsive party?' And passed on. Rimmer nodded agreement into the receding back. But then most of them are. Frozen moments flattened against embassy walls with visiting midge-mite experts, Pioneer Latin professors declining drink, *potio, potionem* . . . the hell with it, midge mite strike on here. He thought of trying to rejoin A N Other, but locating him at some distance talking to a face he again vaguely recalled, decided against it and began to move into the room in short tacks. Finding himself opposite a closed door (bedroom? skippery?) he opened it and prepared to step in.

It was a bedroom. On the bed, nesting in a couple of gowns and a TCD Association scarf, was Miss Cameron. Her eyes were closed. The man with her, bending over, back to the door, had her cami-knickers at least fifty percent . . .

Rimmer retreated, shocked into recall. He had waited until six, the sounds of other people's revelry almost unbearable, until a combination of rage, frustration and despair forced him from the rooms. But then the memory faded. What had he done until it was time to go back for his gown and take his place on a much depopulated Commons, non-party divinity students and downward social climbers? *Un seul hêtre me manqué* . . . Had he drunk the beer, picked at the food and listened without emotion to a medical student, at the pudding stage, informing his course companions that the College had a contract with Aer Lingus for the contents of the sick bags . . . ?

He would go and see his wife.

He took the long way round New Square. Parties were still in progress. In the Park the Races were over, the throng dispersed except for a lone figure in a top hat, uncle Bob's trousers and no shoes, stranded somewhere in the middle of the cricket pitch, happily losing the run of himself. Jealousy. The intensity of it had surprised him. As he walked round by where the new library would be towards the rising scaffolding of the Moyne Institute he ran a quick scan over other betrayals stored in his memory; but all failed to move in him anything but wonder that the deceptions had driven him to drink or near dementia. The close encounters (one already wet from the rival's attentions) now struck him as grotesque, the grand passions—not more than two—as having happened to someone else altogether. Miss Cameron. But then he discovered with some surprise that he was in fact thinking of Barbara, out there in the flat in Ballsbridge staring at the wall. Should he risk the distance, and indeed the time? Would A N Other go back without him? He continued the circuit of the Park, the Pavilion still exuding merriment, a straggle of absorbed couples along the grassy bank at the back of the rugger pitch. *My own Peggy Lee*: the song ebbed and flowed inside his head as if played off a very floppy disc. Then he was through the iron gate, past the Museum Building and approaching the Rubrics. All he had to do was to turn right, find the doorway, mount the stairs . . .

But instead he continued on past the sombre bulk of the Library, the idea forming in his mind of a quiet drink in Jammet's back bar, boys who will be men when I am a man, and dinner for one. Or perhaps. But how could he bring her out for a meal, she who even on good days would almost leap out of her skin at the jangle of cutlery? At least, he thought, he could look into number 4, just to reassure himself that all was as it should be. As he went in the sound of the piano came to him from the room on the left: the same piece, the Brahms, and by all accounts the same pianist, only this time attacking the restatement of the theme with a fury that did not even try to contain the more isolated high notes in the treble. Had he, too, before going back to get the gown for Commons, let himself in, and without the score . . . ?

He turned right into the jacks, counted the cubicles. No one about, no crepitant buckling of Bronco from behind the couple of half-closed doors. Pushing the door of the third cubicle from the end (they had both of them carefully noted it) he went in. The gown, with his old shirt wrapped inside it, was still there, tucked almost out of sight behind the porcelain. The airside door, however, was not. From the room across the hallway came the slam of the piano lid. The bell was tolling for Commons.

8

Benedict Anthony McKinney was a little surprised to find nobody at home. He had expected the oak to be sported, his gown left outside with an apologetic note: *see you on Commons*. At times he felt sorry for his young wife, in the throes of what was obviously a first experience, working at it too hard. On the whole, however, they got on remarkably well, given the differences of age, background and (though this was rarely mentioned) religion. When young Rimmer stumbled out of bed at a quarter to ten on a Sunday morning, groping for his surplice, making a dash to get into Chapel before the bell stopped ringing, he, McKinney, had already returned from Mass in Westland Row. They had rarely discussed their varieties of religious experience, though once the subject had arisen in the context of sexual relationships. It must have been an evening in Hilary term, the damp turf smouldering in the hearth. 'It says here,' McKinney had said, indicating his book, that '"the Catholic is the girl you love so much that she can lie to you, and the Protestant is the girl who loves you so much you can lie to her . . ."'

'Who said that?' asked Rimmer, feigning disinterest. McKinney had turned to the title page, showed it to him. *Nightwood,* Djuna Barnes.

'Never heard of him.'

'Her.'

'*Her.* I don't agree. Not in my case anyway.'

McKinney did not pursue it further. Apart from Miss Cameron, whom he assumed to be a Northern Protestant, Rimmer had hinted occasionally at a girl with some kind of addiction he had met at the Crystal Ballroom. But at the age of twenty-four and with three years of bombing Germany behind him, he felt a natural diffidence at trespassing in the emotional world of someone four years his junior, someone who clearly presumed in him a familiarity with the opposite sex he did not possess. English-born of Irish Catholic parents, he found it difficult to enter the closed circles of Irish Protestantism, as represented minimally by his wife and more encompassingly by the college in which his ex-service grant had somewhat unexpectedly lodged him. Elected, equally unexpectedly, a Scholar of the House, he was schooling himself to recite the grace shorn of Roman intonation (*huius Collegii conditrice,* he believed, would eventually betray him) but had otherwise made little concession to his surroundings. Once a week he would join a gathering of other ex-servicemen in the Buttery in Dawson Street or in Jammet's back bar; but the talk, apart from the obligatory bawdiness, was largely of the difficulty of stretching the grant to the end of the term. Most of them were Irish only by background or association, unspokenly distancing themselves from the Mountjoy schoolboys conducting their tentative romances on the steps of the Reading Room, discussing the hopelessness of life over Carnival Specials in Cafolla's or, on rare occasions, getting maggoty drunk on a tenpenny pint of cider in the Pearl Bar. The reading from Djuna Barnes had thus been as much an effort at bridge-building as anything else.

McKinney, having knocked and waited, let himself in. No unwashed teacups, no aura of a female presence. A half bottle of

Barsac stood unopened on the mantlepiece beside the JD's post-card and a ticket for the D U Choral Society's concert the next day, *The Coffee Cantata*. He went into the skippery, put the kettle on the greasy gas ring, glad that he did not have to go down the stairs again to the solitary tap to fill it. There was a knock at the door. He had not heard any footsteps on the stairs.

Rimmer's nerve had failed him again on the second attempt. He had climbed to the top of number 27 and stood for some moments at the window looking out over the square, still preserving its integrity in the fading evening light. Figures, some weaving unsteadily away from parties, others, the unsocial or unregarded, moving within the framework with the assurance of those happy to play the rules, were too far away, both in space and time, for him to be certain of recognition. Somebody crossing behind the Campanile with what looked like a music-case evoked a momentary shiver of memory, but he was like a figure encountered in a dream, at once familiar and an utter stranger. Against this quietly patterned background he found himself peopling Front Square with figures of his own imagination: friends and acquaintances observed at a safe distance through the wrong end of a telescope. In confronting his wife he would, even with the new forty-year gap in their ages, be confronting himself. Feeling slightly light-headed he went down to their landing and knocked.

'Benedict Anthony McKinney?' The young man with the slightly dropped handlebar moustache looked at him with some uncertainty. But then, disconcerted in his turn, Rimmer found himself addressing him not from the threshold but from the open doorway of what he sensed, rather than identified, as his former bedroom, behind him a smell of damp and furtive nocturnal practices, in front of him, in what appeared for a moment as a fish-eye panoramic shot, the room in all its threadbare comfort; a turf fire smouldering in the grate, the model cottage, once hanging outside the Country Shop, over the fireplace, his wife's assorted football memorabilia, a framed photograph of an RAF bomber squadron, a decorous pinup from some forgotten magazine, installed whether by himself or McKinney he could not remember. The latter seemed not to have observed the dislocation. Some hacker, concluded Rimmer, trying to get in on the act. Perhaps some other passenger has discovered the airside jacks . . . and with another reformulation of spatial dispositions found himself this time standing in the skippery, the oleaginous aroma of generations of incinerated sausages cooked in encrusted pans infrequently sluiced with cold water fixing him imperiously in time if in no other dimension. The solitary teatowel, in service since the beginning of term and used by the skip, in rare onsets of modified enthusiasm, to double as a duster, mocked him with its unassailable reality. McKinney, again apparently unaware of his translation, was still looking at him with the half-amused, quizzical look (product, he had supposed in those times, of a precocious world-weariness), awaiting an explanation of his unstable presence.

'Please come in,' said his former wife, apparently unaware of the fact that Rimmer was now standing by the bookcase absorbing, through the back of his head, a row of titles: *Nightwood,* by Djuna Barnes; *Military Motors of World War One* (McKinney, he remembered, had been an enthusiastic member of the college Motor Cycle and Light Car Club); the *Dublin University Calendar 1949–50*; Butcher's *German Legal Licences T–Z* and a clatter of similar textbooks.

'That's real kind of you, to be sure.' His fake American, beside McKinney's clipped RAF intonation, sounded almost plausible. 'Allow me to introduce myself. Egerton Philip Rimmer, Doctor of Mortuary Science, from Berkeley, California. Though I guess you good people call it Berkeley.'

'You must be . . . ?'

'You've got it in one,' interrupted Rimmer, again uncomfortable with the idiom and only mildly surprised to discover that this time he was speaking from the depths of the intermittently collapsible armchair, in which on occasions he and Miss Cameron . . . 'a distant relation, in more senses than one, I guess, of the Rimmer who is, as I read from the names on the wall down below, your roommate. Perhaps he has spoken of me?'

'Jolly good show,' said McKinney, 'but no, he hasn't actually. There is, if you don't mind my saying so, sir, a quite remarkable family resemblance.'

'Happens occasionally across generations, I guess,' said Rimmer, now finding himself seated on one of the hard chairs, the one with the short leg, at the table on which was the detritus of the monastic Sunday tea—a pot of Lamb's jam, strawberry; butter, bread, an open copy of a College magazine: *She quelled the choking in her throat and turned her taut face towards the pigeons. They stepped precisely and fearlessly over the*—'though in fact we have never met. You might say that this is a surprise visit, ok?' He was back in the armchair again, only this time with a warm if invisible weight in his lap, the tantalizing pressure of a suspender button through a thin frock. Whoever was squawking the wrong transponder codes was playing it meanly.

'Well, I'm sorry he isn't here,' said McKinney, 'no idea where he is, as a matter of fact. Of course, it's Trinity Monday . . .'

'Monday?' interposed Rimmer, discountenanced. College Races? The Sunday tea??

'Wednesday,' McKinney excused himself. 'Not to worry. But Trinity Monday was a big day for me. Scholar of the House against all expectations, those of my Tutor included.' He went through the motions of winding a hand-held cine-camera.

'Congratulations are in order, I guess,' said Rimmer. 'But I wasn't really expecting to find him just dropping in like this. Fact is, I'd have been rather surprised. But since I was passing through . . .'

He was standing over in the corner by the rickety table occupied by the Phillips portable radio as it crackled into life: *On the ground that, as a civilian,* the Pope was saying, *Tone was not subject to punishment by a court-martial. Lord Kilwarden immediately granted the writ. Tone's guilt had been admitted. The judges were inimical to the*—the rest was drowned in interference.

'Gremlins,' said McKinney, coming over and switching it off. 'Pity, he's always worth hearing on what he calls the pathology of democracy.'

'Is that so?' said Rimmer, again from the skippery. Under his feet were the leavings of a load of Lullymore Briquettes which the vanman from Donnelly's in Westmoreland Street had dumped there, confusing the cooking area with the coalhole. But that had been on another occasion surely: conflation once again?

The shifting viewpoint had given him the opportunity to observe his wife in context from a variety of angles. As he looked into the clear blue eyes, unrememberedly childlike over the hirsute lip, he wondered what had become of him. Foundation Scholar and a good legal degree, but a decision not to practise, to head off to, where was it, Canada? Sitting perhaps *stratisque relictis* in the

Athenian Inn in Pike Place Farmers Market in Seattle sipping a Clammy Mary having forsworn the drink after the breakup of . . . but this was speculation. He could read nothing in the face of the young man before him of what he was to become, any more than he, for his part, was disinterring from his own ravaged hair and double-bagged eyes the ever-loving wife of forty years. Suffused by the reticent warmth of that fortuitous and long-distanced camaraderie, he stumbled out of speech into an uncomfortable silence, orchestrated once more from the chair, but this time following an invitation from McKinney to sit down.

'I could give him a message. Can he contact you somewhere?'

'Well, I guess that would be difficult. Yes, sir. The typical American tour of Europe—seven countries in six days' (though were the Americans, he wondered, already into that in 1950?). McKinney appeared to accept it, nevertheless. Though he added: 'My only excuse is that it is university business. Or mostly.' And tried a wink.

But he had forgotten the ingrained vein of what he used to call puritanism in his wife, not altogether accountable to his religion. The book he had come across, when they were both working for Mod. through that long summer, on the table one morning. Had McKinney, in fact, discovered a vocation? The thought made him uncomfortable. Priests in the field he was at ease with, debating the difficulties of drilling well-holes and, having drilled them, persuading the Kibuji to accept and implement the prescribed well-woman counselling. The lids get broken or misused, the water polluted, infection becomes epidemic and the priest abusive with the rest of us. Ireland missed out on its own vocation as a colonial power. We had the habit of command from ecclesiastical sanction—yes, even the Prods—and enough innate racialism to wield it without undue embarrassment. Yet we're doing better as the only Common Market Third World country: we understand whining beggars in the streets; all the stratagems in the move from mountain farm to Mercedes; Spanish arch affluence and public squalor. And we understand how to put a smile in the eyes of stony-faced Kibuji chisellers talking English with Cork accents, how to give the come-uppance to Kibuji gombeen men, how to fill the unforgiving African minutes with eighty-seconds' worth of . . .

'American, did you say? I wouldn't place you from your accent.'

'Born in Ireland, all those years ago,' said Rimmer hastily, 'I guess I haven't altogether lost it.' He should have remembered McKinney's stories of having flown with the Yanks during the war. Sloppy lot, had been his verdict: needed a few press-on types to bring them up to scratch.

'I flew with the Yanks during the war,' McKinney was saying, 'Sloppy lot. Need a few press-on types. But I got to know some of them—Deep South mostly. Accents not at all like yours. Where did you say you were from?'

Rimmer could not remember. 'Oh, I've lived all over.' He held onto the woodwormed arms of the chair, willing himself into immobility.

'Tea?' asked McKinney. 'I've just put the kettle on.'

'Thank you, no. I guess I must be on my way.' The pressure was on his knee again, a subtle shift of warm thighs, hair in his left eye. He rubbed it, to cover his confusion. 'Something in my eye. Would you have a mirror?'

'Of course.' McKinney, the model of neatness and organization, disappeared into the bedroom, returning with a small pocket glass, Rimmer took it, getting out of the chair and immediately finding himself again in the skippery, the kettle steaming softly into the back of his trousers. When he raised the mirror to his face it had misted and he had to wipe it with his sleeve to reassure himself that there was nobody there. The singing of the kettle as it came to the boil prevented him from hearing the door opening and closing quietly.

He returned to the armchair—again, he was pleased to note, of his own volition. The room remained empty. Had his wife left him? Or was he, having extracted the mirror from its carefully calibrated position, simply out there reorganising the bedroom, as had been his wont? Rimmer's untidiness used to disturb him, the RAF training rendering him incapable of comprehending how a random object could be permitted to intrude upon an otherwise allotted airspace: everything in his world came with its programme holding pattern. Thus when McKinney had come upon a packet of French letters lying beside the sugar bowl in the skippery it was not the object itself that upset him or the suspicion that his young wife might, in some rootedly adolescent way, be trying to lay claim to experience to which he was patently a stranger, but the fact that its location was entirely inappropriate. Nothing, of course, was said. Their evolved system of living together, drawn in each case from an equal, if not similarly-derived diffidence, was to relapse into silence like, Rimmer had thought at the time, an old married couple. The thought, he was to discover with the decades, was a facile assumption of youth and, a number of years later, gasping for air in the choking silence of a fading marriage, he had looked back wistfully to those evenings on each side of the smoking fire when one interrogative 'tea?' at ten forty-five could focus an embalming placidity of which, until that point, he had hardly been aware. Once in the chill darkness of his own bedroom, however, it was another matter. The sagging springs received him as if in an obscene embrace, the images of Miss Cameron, Barbara, and the strange, transparent-bloused girl he had sat behind in a very boring lecture in the first weeks of his first term . . .

'Who she?' he had pencilled, with a well-directed arrow, to the quiescent neighbour with whom he had struck up an early and quickly dissipated acquaintanceship. And the latter, with the lecturer's eye roving around them like that of a dilatory sheepdog, had cautiously pencilled back THE CAT'S MOTHER. A nymphomaniac, they had whispered in schoolboy glee of the Cat's Mother; and Rimmer, sniggering with the rest, had had to go and look it up in the Reading Room. That definition, *characterised by morbid and uncontrollable sexual desire* had tormented him. As for its verification or otherwise (she had lost her year and . . .)

Rimmer once more looked round the room. Often he had confronted its dream-image, waking in some steaming littoral night with the tolling of the Campanile bell revealing itself as the insistent attention of a mosquito, sweating with the sensation of once-familiar objects arbitrarily disordered (he must, after all, have learnt something from McKinney), the walls painted crimson. Now, however, it all looked irreally normal, so much so that any sense of revisitation was virtually negatived by the commonality of continuous experience. But where the hell was McKinney? He looked at his watch: though now ticking, its hands remained motionless. He got up and went over to the window from which he used to be able to see the clock at Front Gate. He could see the clock, but his eyesight was no longer good enough to read it.

Front Square was empty, the parties over, the shuttered silence descending, underscored by the distant ground bass of traffic in Pearse Street. Glad to find himself still in one place at a time he turned to the door as the steps which seemed to be making heavy weather of ascending the staircase stopped outside it. Must have been down to the jacks. Would always slip out with that curious modesty. Searchlights over Hamburg.

But it was not McKinney. Rimmer had always disliked, in clothes shops and similar places, catching sight of himself in a triple mirror. Say, could that cad be I, all slithy grin and stubble? It always was. And now.

Himself, not troubling to put on the light, was crossing the room, heavy-footed, flinging the music-case onto the table. Rimmer had his back to the window, his face in deep shadow.

'You're looking for McKinney, I suppose. How did you get in?'

'McKinney let me in. He's just slipped down to the jacks I think.' Neither Rimmer's statement, nor the de-Americanised voice in which it was delivered, created any impression. In 1950, of course, I would never have heard myself. Even so . . . and then the explanation dawned on him: the man was drunk. Scuttered. It came back across the years more clearly: the walking of the streets that ended in the Pearl and how many self-pitying pints before a return to grab the music, skip Commons and take it out on Brahms and that oversprung Collard & Collard. Wasn't that it? She grew into a fat granny, the Cat's Mother. Or so I heard.

'Who are you? I'm afraid I'm . . . I'll put on the light.'

'No, not for just a minute.' Rimmer was before him to the light switch, the geography informing the arthritic fingers. Himself turned unsteadily on his heel and fell heavily into the chair, which seemed to be on the point of resolving itself into discrete components. For a moment neither spoke. Through the window, which Rimmer had pushed up the better to attempt to read the clock, there floated the incongruous melody of 'Linden Lee' sung by a male voice group apparently stationed under the Campanile. As they leaned down low a window in the Graduates' Memorial Building opened and some object, projected by a music-hater, or perhaps a music-lover, clattered against the stonework. The song ceased.

'I'm sorry,' said Himself. 'I'm feeling rather ill.'

Rimmer became aware of the acrid taste of the Tanzanian rosé on his tongue. He looked anxiously at the figure in the chair, reluctant now to assert his presence to the point where Himself would recall it as other than a drunken illusion, product of frustration and misery. He found his mind locking again into the closed circle, *if I was not here then I cannot be here now.* But what did I, in that drunken, jealous depression of 1950, remember of the night of that—or this—Trinity Wednesday and a figure speaking out of the darkness? He tried to summon some estimate of the degree of drunkenness (he had been, after all, very much the novice) but it was the misery, rather than the alcohol, that was coming over to him from the chair. Should he tell what he knew? The party, the cami-knickers fifty percent . . . ?

'Try Jammet's back bar. He drinks there sometimes when he's flush with the ex-service types. Now if you'll excuse me I think I'll go to bed.'

Rimmer watched. Images of his own son suffering his first hangover, his first rebuttal, mingled with a growing anger at the drooped figure in the chair. Was I so awkward, so ungainly, so sorry for myself? The sports coat, of a shade and style almost identical with the one he had just bought in Kevin & Howlin's, was rumpled and, though he could not see them in the gloom, probably emblazoned with canteen medals. Here was the seed of everything he had subsequently brought upon himself. *Economics, Dr Chubb and Dr Lyons. Answer four questions. Do we recruit our higher civil servants in the most efficient manner possible? If not, what improvement or methods do you suggest? Write on at least one side of the paper.*

Rimmer was still by the window, maintaining the precaution of remaining in shadow, but as Himself appeared to slump even further into the greasy cushions, lacking even the motivation to get himself to bed, he felt himself moving towards him, closing the gap. He tried to put himself into reverse, shoes scrabbling the threadbare carpet, but it was like trying to walk the wrong way up an escalator. In a moment we will be face to face. He will rouse himself, peer up, and see . . .

It was worse than that. The sensation was like awakening from a general anesthetic, of being dragged back from the edge of a precipice. I imagined it all, he concluded: Himself was never here at all. Just a projection of me as indeed I . . .

But then he saw the figure standing over by the window. The face was in shadow but the slightly drooping stance, the disposition of the arms were as he had seen them in a score of photographs taken with the village headman, the Departmental headhunter, the boys in the band. Then he looked down. The sports coat of similar cut and cloth but emblazoned with canteen medals, the unpressed grey flannels, acrid with age, cheap Tyler's shoes. He felt the face: smooth, no wrinkles. The hair: thick, bushy, in need of cutting. But the head was clear and on the tongue the lingering aftertaste of the Tanzanian . . .

The figure by the window, who had been standing with his back to him looking out, now moved unsteadily, teetering for a moment off-balance before determinedly if erratically making for the door. He did not look in Rimmer's direction nor offer any indication that he was aware of any other presence in the room. The slam of the inner door was followed by the half-click of the oak only partially closing. 'Linden Lea' echoed on the night, coming now from the direction of an open upper window in the GMB. Rimmer, or what remained of him, sat in stunned silence, trying to assess the situation. Think. Of the erosion in the Hololo Valley. Yes. Of the girls, a short list, he had long ago left behind him. They assumed identities, a mole on a bottom, a distaste for gin. OK. More recently? *Today I saw up her skirt. Cami-knickers fifty percent.* Yes. All but the outward and visible signs. He moved cautiously, stood up. The legs were almost uncontrollably springy, as if he were about to take off like a kangaroo. The fingers, freed of arthritis, twitched involuntarily over ambitious arpeggios. He ran them in wonder through the luxuriant if grubby hair, smoothed the silky-stubbly cheek. Need a shave. That old Rolls razor you ran up and down the strop—never could get it sharp. One facet, however, seemed at odds with the rest. He had observed, flicking through his abridged catalogue of women, one or two who had presented themselves in varying states of readiness, but there had been no response where it might have been expected. He experienced a fleeting moment of regret, but the relief at not having to relive the last forty years from start to finish was overwhelming. Had the exchange been complete he would now have a sick headache, an empty stomach and a broken heart. He would be dragging himself from the chair, gulping the last of the milk and heading for the damp, fusty bedroom, the sagging springs and . . .

Except—and it now came back to him with acute awareness—that was not the way it had been at all. With the refracted clarity of drunkenness he had decided that there was still something to be salvaged from the wreck of the day. He had stood looking out the window, fingers probing the faults in the eighteenth-century woodwork as he had sought its support. Fuck Miss Cameron—a word he then rarely used even to himself. The mnemonic (mnemonic for what he had since forgotten) running through his head: *Barbara, Celarent, Darii, Ferio . . . what is logic, by the by? Science of the form of thinking. Here the bacon starts to fry.* Barbara.

This, thought Rimmer, with something approaching panic, will have to be stopped. An elderly gentleman with a scuttered student inside him slouching towards Ballsbridge to . . . slamming both doors behind him he took the stairs one at a time.

9

'It sounds to me a little far-fetched,' said A N Other.

Strolling gently across Parliament Square in the general direction of number 4 he had responded to Rimmer's summons but turned to look blankly at the young man who stood before him, dishevelled, unshaven and seemingly the prey to some strong emotion.

'It's me, Other,' said a voice that was indisputably that of Rimmer and equally indisputably issuing from the figure before him. 'Something terrible's happened.'

A N Other for the moment said nothing, subjecting the pseudo-Rimmer to a close inspection.

'Yes,' he admitted, 'I can see the likeness. You weren't bad looking in a messy kind of way. If you hadn't lost most of the hair, I'd have twigged you at once. That and the middle-age spread.'

Rimmer was too concerned to take offence. 'You don't recognise me?'

'Of course I recognise you. Haven't I just said so?'

'No, I mean you don't recognise me from then—I mean now?'

A N Other looked at him closely again. 'Now that you mention it, I seem to have some recollection of you as a figure glimpsed occasionally, and from a distance, around College. Perhaps on Commons—I couldn't be sure after all these years. But that does not necessarily mean that you are not what you seem to be. If that matters. Perhaps you had better explain.'

Rimmer did his best to account for the events of the evening, but his narrative, even to himself, lacked conviction, and he was not surprised at A N Other's remaining sceptical. Only after he had subjected him to an impromptu catechism: *Tanzanian? Rosé. Mooneys? Burgundy. Cami-knickers . . . ?* that he professed himself satisfied that he was not dealing with some more devious kind of changeling.

'Perhaps in the circumstances we had better withdraw to number 4,' he concluded. 'Things are getting a little beyond the beyonds.'

They had been circling Parliament Square, feet clicking reassuringly on the cobbles, talking quietly, so that Rimmer's sense of panicked urgency had subsided into a queasy uneasiness. In the deepening dusk he was now comfortably inside himself, enjoying the spring in his step and the tautness of his stomach muscles. But A N Other's suggestion brought him up short.

'But I can't,' he said, 'don't you see? I'm out there on the loose, a sheep in wolf's clothing, waiting for a number 8 bus. And I've gone off with the travel bag.'

The last time it had happened had been in the Sudan. Out in a village, which had detached itself from a mirage of green trees only when they were upon it, he had left the bag, or its predecessor, on the sand while being politely conducted on a tour of inspection. It was not until he was back in Wad Medani that he had registered the loss. Passport, tickets, travellers' cheques, notes, papers, credit cards . . . you cannot telephone to a village in a mirage. The local field director and his transport were already on the way south. He had been lying awake in the lidded heat wondering where to begin to reconstruct his identity from an open series of variables when there was a gentle knock at the door and a smiling Arab, nobody he recognised, handed him the bag intact. Nothing like that was going to happen now.

The walk to Front Gate, short as it was, was unnerving. A couple of his former contemporaries, looming up from under the lamps, appeared about to accost him until the sight of the elderly figure of A N Other at his side deflected them. The porter greeted him affably: 'Night, Mr Rimmer,' and he replied in a voice he tried to lighten and purge of its forty years' accretions and with something he hoped was an appropriate and in-character observation. Had he held onto the diary he had kept intermittently of his time in College something might have stuck, a page flipped open and scanned, half with interest, when packing which he could now summon to the reconstruction of what was to follow. But it had never amounted to much more than a pallid record of interstices, the spaces between the spokes and he had thrown it out of a porthole and into the Red Sea as they crawled through at four knots on his first voyage out. The putting away of childish things. To his embarrassment not only had it floated but was retrieved by a young swimmer who now, fat old Port Said camel hirer (or, with the passing of the liners, are there any tourists to be photographed on their backs?) might only yesterday have come across it again while looking for something else altogether and was now sitting over a doll's house cup of coffee laboriously spelling out the fragment account of a stranger in a strange . . .

Sensing his unease, A N Other stopped outside the gate and began reading in a confidential monotone from a magazine he had been carrying rolled up like a night-stick: *The motion was proposed by Mr Grant of the Speculative Society of Edinburgh, who claimed that the Past was not a logical process, and that we must always expect the unexpected. The case for the Negative was put first by Mr Southall of the Durham Union, who sought to find the relation of the Past to the Present. He came to the conclusion that our past implies our present, and that our actions are the result of conditioning in the Past. Mr Rees-Mogg of the Oxford Union found that, though the past belongs to us . . .*

The actuality of this Trinity Wednesday. Had he in fact exchanged a greeting with the porter, had he . . . ?

He was followed by Mr St John Stevas of the Cambridge Union, who made, perhaps, the most constructive speech of the evening. He claimed that the way we take into the future is our own choice . . .

Water stains, forty years in the desert . . . Had he waited for this bus? Or thought better of it, gone dejectedly back to bed?

'Where did you get that?' he asked A N Other.

'I removed it from the Hist. Luckily nobody there I knew. But then I was only an active member for a term or two. Other interests prevailed.'

'Removal of magazines, even College magazines, was frowned upon.'

'If I removed it, it had been removed. Or, to put it another way, destined for removal.'

'By your young self?'

'It is possible. Unlike you, Rimmer, I have no real recollection of the day that's in it. But then as far as I am concerned the matter is scarcely crucial.'

For the first time it struck him that A N Other might be planning to desert him. Nothing easier than to hang back as he boarded the rear platform of the bus and, before he could jump off at the next stop, somewhere down Nassau Street, hightail it to number 4 and back through the airside door where, in his present guise, he could scarcely dare to follow. 'I must pull myself together,' he said out loud.

'Exactly. Your man has a head start on you. That is, if he went. Try to remember. If you can't catch up with him there is, as I see it, precious little chance of your getting your act together.'

'I remember,' said Rimmer, 'lying on the floor of the flat after a hopeless attempt to make her tell me where she had got the drugs if they were drugs, her standing over me, whether accidentally or on purpose. Cami-knickers fifty percent. But it could have been another evening altogether. One way or another I have to get there first. Imagine . . .'

'I would rather not,' said A N Other primly. 'On the other hand you might just have gone for a drink. If the bus isn't here in five minutes I suggest we do that anyway.'

'I would have thought I had had enough for one night—though Himself seems to have taken his hangover with him. Anyway, the pubs are shut'—the clock over Front Gate was showing just after ten—'or as near as dammit. And'—he felt his pockets—'I seem to have no money. *He* has my money,' he added indignantly, 'or, rather, yours.'

'Think nothing of it,' said A N Other, 'my fifteen pounds is still intact. What else is in those pockets? It might give us a clue.'

Rimmer felt inside the jacket and extracted a battered wallet. 'I don't know whether . . .'

'Don't be ridiculous. It's yours, after all. You needn't show me anything personal.'

By the light of the streetlamp, Rimmer examined the contents.

No money. 'That's strange. I used to always keep a pound for dire emergencies.'

'You spent it, remember?'

'I remember. On the half bottle of Barsac and the Bewley's cake. There must have been some change, surely.'

'Sundry predators. What else is there?'

Rimmer further investigated the paltry contents. Two used half-tickets for the Regal Rooms Cinema. Membership card of the Westmoreland Home Rule Society, given to him by his wife. (He had never discovered where Westmoreland was and when he went to look, years later, it had vanished without trace). A couple of Reading Room slips.

'Nothing,' he said. 'What did you expect? An invitation to an exhibition and private view?'

10

'It gets darker earlier.'

'And it's colder too,' said Rimmer. He shivered.

'We could always go inside. You look delicate.'

'I suppose because I'm younger. At least I presume I'm younger. This is one of those things that transports you . . .'

'I wish you hadn't started thinking about it, much less reminiscing. There we were all set to get the bus. Where are we?' A N Other peered out over the rail in front of him. 'At least we're on the right line.'

'That's what did it. How does it go? *Something that moves in determinate grooves, not a bus, not a bus but a . . .*'

'Precisely. I suppose,' he said gloomily, 'it must now be around 1948.'

'Not much earlier,' agreed Rimmer, 'there's a few cars around, so definitely post-Emergency. But would you look at the cut of me.' He examined himself with some interest. 'Same clothes. Same'— he checked the pocket—'wallet. Same contents.' The light in the open front balcony of the tram was barely enough to see by. Two half-tickets for the Regal Rooms Cinema (wonder who I went with? And when?). Membership card of the Westmoreland . . .

'Used you always carry so little about your person?'

'No, now that I come to think of it. I have the magpie temperament, damn nuisance when you're constantly on the move.' *Tickets for the Paris sewers. Wrapper from a Raspberry Fruity manufactured by Lemon & Company, Dublin. Ticket for the Passing Out Dance of the 31 Platoon at the Vienna Woods Hotel (most of them did). Kriebel's Bath-Kitchen Boutique and Gift Shoppe, Maple Avenue & Main Street, Dublin PA. Newspaper cutting, faded, of Mrs Irene Laycock wearing protective clothing as she brings slabs of spaghetti from the deep freeze.* 'An inveterate fragment-shorer.'

'A what?'

'But to answer your question, no.'

'Then the wallet?'

'Of course.' Rimmer sounded relieved. 'Discarded, with the redolent coat—tweed is apparently at its most absorbent when the bacon starts to fry—God knows when. I, I mean Himself, must have dug it out of the back of the wardrobe in the bedroom as a suitable complement to the squalor of his emotional circumstances.' It was all, he was pretending, so unimaginably different.

'So it can tell us nothing,' concluded A N Other. 'This Dalkey tram will, unless I am way off the beam, take us via Ballsbridge. Do we get off? When did your liaison with this, er, Barbara commence?'

'I wish I could tell you. Good evening, my name is Rimmer. I wonder would it be convenient to start doing a line with you, say, sometime in 1949? Good, then I'll see you in the Crystal Ball . . . But what's the point? Himself could still be out there where we left him in 1950. I'd only put the wind up the poor girl—and in her state that was never very difficult.'

The tram clanked past the genteel wilderness of Merrion Square, lurched with a flash from the trolley into Lower Mount Street. The door from the interior saloon opened, emitting an evanescent odour of the unwashed and a cheery conductor.

'Two to Ballsbridge,' said A N Other firmly.

An inbound number 8 swayed towards them, enclosed luxury car, passed with a gentle susurration of the trolley and a lightly-oiled eddy of wind. Rimmer shivered again, experiencing a sudden yearning for the desperate Tanzanian, the equivocal promise of the airport menu, the reassurance of being able to do nothing. Suppose Barbara did answer the door and recognised him, a feat she had managed only intermittently during their relationship? He would have no idea at what point to resume, whether to sit on a chair or lie on the floor. Whatever happened to suburban sex-offenders in 1948? They certainly never appeared in the unsocial columns of *The Irish Times*. There had been a coinbox telephone up in the hall. *Operator, I'm being looked up at, at least fifty percent, by a senile Trinity student who claims he met me next year in the . . .*

'How did you get on? I mean, at the party. I lost sight of you.'

'Luckily there were very few there I might once have known,' said A N Other, 'and I kept well out of their way. It wasn't too difficult in the crush. But it is extraordinary, now that you think of it, how one accepted one's own closed circle, even in a place as intimate as Trinity, as the whole academic world. So much so that I began to wonder whether some of those I didn't recognise weren't themselves blow-ins.'

'Blow-ins? Gate-crashers, like ourselves?'

'Like ourselves, exactly. After all, if we can simply walk through an airside jacks . . .'

'I wondered the same thing about a cow I once met tied to a tree on the island of Pemba. I was scared to turn my back on her in case when I turned round again she wouldn't be there at all.

Perhaps Barbara, too, was a blow-in. Perhaps it wasn't drugs at all but a vertiginous oscillation of time-zones that had her the way she was. But I suppose we had better get off.'

They alighted at the Lansdowne Road kiosk, watched the tram clatter away into the gloom. Standing hunched against the chill, Rimmer again became acutely conscious of his anomalous constitutional condition. Like a *bombe surprise*. The outside, the eighteen-year-old integument, never having yet, he reflected, experienced the debilitating effects of tropical heat, or indeed, anything over twenty-three degrees, was revelling in the conditions, hair undulating lumpily on the breeze like a scruffy petted cat, nostrils narrowed enough to pass through the eye of a camel. No one, then—now—had ever set foot in a Spanish summer. Summer was goosepimples, gooseberries with his elder brother in the bungalow in Tramore. Inwardly, however, he was shuddering. Himself plunging disparately, half-cut, somewhere around the city, trying to infuse fire into that sixty-year-old tub of guts, aghast, without knowing why, at the tatter of lank hair, the folds of flab, the knees tending to collapse like superannuated Tramore deckchairs. If he were to fall off a stool, now, in the Bailey . . . A clatter of coatless, weaving figures struggling up from the direction of the rugby ground. Late celebrators of some match or other, win or lose . . .

'I'll be seeing you,' said A N Other with sharp decision, 'twenty-three hundred by Trinity clock, not a minute later. *Kwa heri.* And good luck.'

'You're going?' Rimmer, suspicious again, tried to make the question sound casual.

'My dear man, you would scarcely expect me to play gooseberry at my time of life. And, to be brutally frank, I am finding the company of an elderly eighteen-year-old somewhat disconcerting, to put it mildly. I doubt if I could even bring you into a pub.'

'They're closed. And if that's the way you look at it, lend me a pound. No, make it two. If it won't leave you short.'

A N Other handed over the notes without comment. 'Matter of fact I only came this far for the ride. To fill in time, whatever that means in this context. It's been rather a fiasco, don't you know. What have we done but drink and gate-crash a stupid party? The past is not all it's cracked up to be.'

'Agreed. There's no time like the present.'

'The past is, I suppose, not a logical process, and we must always expect the unexpected. I might even bump into Mogg and Stevas.'

'Don't go into any strange jacks. You might find yourself in a passage to India.'

'There are worse places,' said A N Other. 'I shall hope to catch a bus back. To 1950. Heaven preserve us from starting to live backwards.'

'Not a bus, not a bus, but a pram. I agree. And if there are two of us, if you follow me, at Front Gate . . .'

'You aren't thinking of bringing that woman?'

'Good lord, no. If there are two of us make sure, for goodness' sake, that you pick the right one. If in doubt, bring the one that looks senescent on the outside. I can always learn to grow old gracefully.'

'I doubt it. When you get back to Dublin—I mean properly back to Dublin—they'll diagnose infantile regression and, with luck, offer you early retirement. Your wife will be in for a surprise.'

'He was. *Kwa heri.* And don't let me down.'

'I won't. But if for any reason I'm not there, or if you don't make it until after eleven, try to get back on your own. I'll keep you some of the Tanzanian and a leg of piggin—unless, of course, the flight is called.'

'Come back like this?'

'No, of course not. Think yourself back into 1950—my guess is that your man is still around, and will be only too happy to change faces with you. And forget the trams.'

'Something rather romantic happened to me once on the top of a tram in Hong Kong.'

'I might have guessed. I'll leave you, so.' He strode off in the direction of the city, not looking back.

'Excuse me,' said an unsteady figure, about his own external age, in a green and white paper hat, 'would you ever have a light?' Did I smoke? he tried to remember, groping in the pockets. Not in this old coat anyway.

'Sorry,' he said, aiming once more at a youthful intonation, 'Who won?'

The figure looked him up and down in amazement. 'Who won, is it? Ireland 14–5. Bloody marvellous. Kyle and Strathdee.'

'I was travelling. May I see?' With the audacity of elderly youth he took hold of the programme half-crumpled in the young man's pocket: *Ireland v England Lansdowne Road Saturday February 12, 1949. Kick-off 3 p.m. elVERYs are GOOD for Rugger Supplies.* No wonder it's cold. And dark. But at least time is moving in the right direction. Maybe I should be taking the floor. He returned the programme, unopened, into the hands of the astonished supporter and set off, spring in his step, up Pembroke Road, wishing that Himself had had the decency to shave.

11

On Raglan Road on an autumn day I met her first and knew . . . He turned the corner, ducking his head against the onset of a light rain and watched the cracks between the paving slabs calibrate his unrelentingly athletic footsteps. Elgin Road was as he had always remembered it, the Victorian houses standing back disdainfully, most, even in the Fifties, already fallen into flats, bedsitters with haphazardly carpentered hardboard walls dividing once spacious rooms, reluctant plumbing crammed into erstwhile pantries, the smell of small fries. The vividness of the recollection alarmed him, as did his growing internal acquiescence in the physical imperatives of his exterior. Were the two coalescing, mind following body? He tried slowing the step, summoning the waiter/cashier, recollecting details of the menu. A face swam up, but it took on the physiognomy of one Dammo Camillia (he wasn't sure about the first name), the unpredictable Italian who had opened the restaurant somewhere off the Quays and either threw plates at his customers or serenaded them with the upper half of the 'Vorrei far pulire' duet from Verdi's *Endomice*. But the place ('off-quay Camillia's,' as it came to be known) had surely closed thirty years ago, perhaps even before he had left Ireland for the first time. He had taken Barbara there for a birthday, but it had been a plate night, a disaster. At the first crash she had toppled off her chair in what he had thought to be a coma so that Camillia, coffee-saucer aimed at the cash-register, had broken off in mid-recoil. *He looked up my skirt in his Italian dictionary.* They left

amid contrite apologies and the glimmering first notes of 'Vorrei.'
Walking more slowly was now demanding a real effort of will, as
he tried to slot in something that would assure him of really having lived to sixty. Turning the corner, head even lower as the rain
intensified, he saw the pair of red shoes.

The drive in from the airport in a new city: the utter strange-
ness, a shout in the street, spice from a market stall, a poster for
the Midnat Club Live Show All Included KR25. Knowing that in
thirty minutes, room 357, thank you sir, enjoy your stay, sniffing
out the territory, tail erect at the prospect of an expense-account
evening in the Midnat Club, already a temporary citizen, instant
familiarity, illusion of belonging, of having been here before. So
with the shoes, and the foreknowledge, or memory of what was
to come. Ten paces on a green dralon blouse, not yet viscid with
the rain. The grey skirt followed, some heavy material, scrunched
as if discarded in a hurry. He had never had any real awareness
of clothes, and remembered stopping then as he stopped now, in
an agony of doubt as to whether these were like anything she had,
to his knowledge, ever worn. No, he had concluded. And then,
three or four steps later, almost kicked in under an overgrowing
hedge, the slip, girdle with the suspenders and stockings still at-
tached and . . .

Rimmer's heart was pounding (a sixty-year-old heart, he was
almost relieved to acknowledge), the prurience of the rediscov-
ery overlaid by the awareness of an action completed before it
had begun. This was for real. All this had happened, enacted on
that same divan or bed. He had quickened his pace, not knowing
whether he hoped or feared to find her crouching naked at her
basement door, victim of assault from either without or within.

But as he reached the gate in the iron railings giving onto the descending stone steps slimy with the rain, there was no one. Then or now.

... *I met her first and knew / That her dark hair would weave a snare that I might one day rue.* Kavanagh, glimpsed once in her company, hunched and giving out, in Mooney's or somewhere. Knew it once by heart. He hesitated, walked on past the gate, took refuge under a dripping tree. Striptease without a body—the titillation now as before. He kicked the tree with a youthful foot, sending a stab of disabling pain into his groin. Thinking he could rise to the occasion. Red shoes no drawers. He turned and was down the steps before he realised it, knocking.

The silence diminished him. But she had never answered the first knock, plunging him, in those days, into telescoped agonies of fear and suspicion. Then the slow step, almost a shuffle, fingers fumbling with the catch like a *Beano* burglar, mask and stripey gansey, cracking a safe haven. Followed by the minimal aperture, through which the eyes . . .

The eyes he would have known—dark, distended pupils—had he seen them any time in the recent present peering out of a dark Kibuji face in a darker hut in a deserted village. Almost the first girl he ever kissed, it had been with his own eyes wide open, fearful of dropping his guard before that unwinking, unfocussed gaze. She opened the door fully, saying nothing. No invitation, no greeting—simply a turn on the heel and a retreat down the minimal hallway with its ziggurat ceiling shaped by the underside of the steps up to the main house and its pervasive smell of damp (long before air-restorers) to the single room, the divan or bed, the gas ring he was fearful she would forget to turn off, the appurtenances of a life which showed very little above the surface. Her possessions had given no clue, and now, as he followed her into the room, grateful for the silence as giving him some chance to position himself closer, but not too close, in time, he caught sight of himself—or he could only presume it was his present self—in the mirror which, hung over the tiny grate, did its best to give the cubbyhole some kind of liveable dimension. Rimmer was startled to observe what looked very like a smirk of self-confidence on the youthful features, whereas his senescent self—still, apparently, inhumed—could prefigure nothing. Calendar on the wall for 1948. But perhaps it had been kept beyond its time for the Paul Henry picture of a mountain he could not, then, believe in, never having set foot in the west.

'Barbara,' he said, as much to hear himself speak, the chance to tighten or slacken a string. Used they kiss? What was expected of him? Passion? Acrimony? Tea?

I would never have made an archaeologist, fiasco at Four Knocks. He carried the kettle into the tiny scullery. Sift through the debris of forty years and come up not with the headlines from the top storeys but the basement anecdotes. How to coax the lid off the caddy. The mechanics of spooning. She sat in the one armchair, eyes like calipers on him as his fingers unravelled the ritual. Her silences had always had to be translated, only now he did not know where to start looking for the crib. Were they at the beginning of the relationship—the slight formality, the as-yet-untempered sexual tensions? Her manner of admitting him had suggested no great empathy, though he sensed having been expected. Perhaps a meeting arranged to continue or counteract a previous evening's encounter? Or perhaps—waiting for the plaintive whistle of the kettle he used to cut off as quickly as possible before it inhibited the atmosphere with loneliness—perhaps we are two years into it, bonds forged exhibiting the first, faint traces of mental fatigue. But not the end. She would have slammed it in my face.

He carried the small circular tray, everything here minimal, back into the room and set it on the erected ironing board.

'Did I interrupt you?'

'No.' But she had been ironing when I took the floor. Is that what is to happen? That I cannot do. But if I did.

'Last night,' she said. 'That man looked like a beleaguered parrot.'

When, as he came to know, but not then, she had been injecting, or swallowing, her words would, without warning, lose themselves in labyrinths in which he had to struggle to identify a nodal reference. The parrot—it had fled him, mockingly, down the years—might have been someone sitting beside them at the *Coffee Cantata*. Music, he had discovered by trial and error, was one of the few experiences she could absorb without panic. Or it might have been afterwards—the drag-footed waitress in Cafolla's: sex-changes were not uncommon. With patience and some insight her words would usually slot themselves into meaning, tea would be taken, buttons pressed activating the desired response. Often, though, the first pot would have been cold before the parrot had been caged. Challenged, tentatively, over a fresh brew she would not acknowledge that it had ever been beleaguered.

'But you look different. Are you all right?'

The reversion to normality alarmed him, as did the queasy acknowledgement of his usurping presence in the mirror. Myself as others saw me.

'I'm grand, Barbara. Shagged. (Would I have said that?) It's been a hard day's night.'

The solecism sailed over her. She took his monastic life apart from her for granted, evincing so little curiosity that he had soon given up attempting to interest her in the academic bath-house rituals, the egg-hurling contests after Commons and other manifestations of the intellectual life. Protestant and student, Catholic and . . . and what? He had never been able to account for what he saw in her, which was why, he supposed, that even now faint stirrings of jealousy were afflicting him like mild indigestion. No stomach for it. And Himself in the Bailey, ravaged and randy? Arrested under two different auspices for aggravated assault and confined in Grangegorman under two different assumed names for the terms of my unnatural life. Perhaps it was the last forty years that was, is, the illusion. Am I meant now to resume where I left off, fall to the floor at her feet? On first looking into Barbara's. Ironing in the soul.

'How was the match?' she enquired calmly, unfolding from the peg-basket an uncompromising garment, green dralon, modest at neck and sleeve.

'Great. We won. Kyle and Strathdee were magic.'

'Were what?'

Wrong slang. He used to tease her with boarding-school words: dodges/bread. Something like that. So many slangs since.

'Magic.' He decided to persist.

'You're late enough.'

So he had been expected. What kind of excuse should he offer? Turn the clock back to 18. Pints? No money. Had he gone back for Commons? To Cafolla's with odd acquaintance Flaherty? But

Flaherty, as he remembered, had despised rugby as a capitalist imposition, though he had had a better word for it. Used to tear up his *Daily Worker* and leave it in a neat pile in the jacks, hoping that something would rub off.

'Anything on the wireless?' Secondhand, full of booming seascapes like his own.

'I didn't get the paper.' Bent over the ironing she looked so unaware that he felt as if his tired old heart needed hoovering. He glanced again at the mirror, fearing a visible change. Dorian greying. The cur-like grin came back at him. Go on, take the floor.

'More tea, Barbara?'

'Yes, please. It was good last night.'

What? The *Coffee Cantata?* The scene on the divan or bed? Danny Kaye at the Theatre Royal? Disturbing the dust in a bowl of tealeaves.

'Your man and the parrot.'

Meanly, and with the sick foreknowledge of many betrayals, enough guilt for a kilo of gingerbread, he saw the way out. All those times he had tried to lure her back to logic, to slip into the interstices the rational element that would rebalance the equation. The strategy had been instinctive, adopted initially in self-defence against the non-logical world into which he was frightened that he, too, might fall. But the drug, whatever it was, assisted him in that it appeared to be spasmodic in effect, islands emerging upon which he would beach himself with shaky relief, quickly making tea, hoping to hold her by the ritual. Now, however, his motives were of the basest. He took a step towards the ironing-board, adolescent arms reached for her whilst his old heart recoiled.

'The parrot,' he said, 'was in paroxysms.'

'I talked to the man. He said he had caught it in Africa. He sold it to the restaurant and they cooked it in red wine. He said it tasted like piggin. What's that?'

'What was this man like?'

'An old man. Like a professor. You should know.'

'Did he talk Latin?'

'Latin? Sure and why would he? Parrots don't . . .'

Very cautiously, impelled by the eighteen-year-old lips, he kissed her. She responded as he had disremembered, whole body trembling, eyes wide, a sudden dart of the tongue like a frog trying to jump out of a jampot. Sickly smell of incest. Further than this he could not, would not, go. But the arms moved round her again, prehensile fingers plotting straps. In spite of himself the eager, muscled legs pressed against her thigh, moving her resistingly backwards towards the divan or bed. Further than this he would not, could not . . .

'I told him about you. He said he had been in Trinity College when he was young but didn't remember anyone called Rimmer. And it's such a funny name.'

They were over now by the divan or bed, the back of her knees against the russet covering. All he had to do now was increase the angle of incidence. But with a start she went rigid, shaking like a battered testament shedding its leaves.

'At the door!'

'I heard nothing.' Then he became aware of it, the doorbell reverberating dully like a stultified angelus, clammy Mary pray for us.

'Leave it. Don't go.'

'I must go. It's the man who said he didn't know you. Hide in the kitchen till he's gone.'

'Pretend you're not here.' His young arms held her, but she wrestled free and ran, cannoning into the ironing-board which fell numbingly into the tiny grate. He picked it up, tried unsuccessfully to induce it to open its legs, propped it precariously against the wall, deciding to stand his ground. Two hours cooped up in the scullery whilst a gentleman caller . . . jealousy stirred again, distant as the first doublings of Santa. He took up a position in the middle of the room so that he could see the door, and beyond it the vestigial hallway, reflected in the mirror. He heard the front door open, a mumble of words in a voice that sounded familiar, close. A N Other fussing about getting back—though he had not remembered giving him the address. He watched her coming back into the room, eyes glazed like that day out on Bray Head when the whistle of a train below had pinned her, terrified, to the rock. Behind her . . .

Nobody. And in the moment it took him to turn from the non-reflexion to the proximate reality the visitor had fled, dragging footsteps down the hallway, the front door opened and slammed. Barbara had fallen back against the wall by the door to the room, eyes unseeing. As he passed her she curled back into herself like flame-shrunk plastic. *Kyle and Strathdee, play for me.* Himself had about a hundred metres' start.

Lights behind tall windows in the stepped-back houses. Secure in their time, faded gentilities not yet usurped, delivered on credit from Findlater's and Lipton's, six adorable kittens require good Protestant homes. He moved easily—*mens insana in corpore* as A N Other would have put it were he here—playing tag with the dim figure ahead of him, cutting corners, Clyde Road, Wellington

Road, Wellington Lane, Waterloo Road—the Gaelic versions on the green enamel nameplates doing nothing, with their humble phonetic approximations, to parry the planter's punch. But where was all this leading? In spite of his spry young legs he was not appreciably gaining. What can he be doing to that poor old body of mine, rheumatical legs flailing through the clammy air, paunch flummering like an exhausted balloon. As the resentment built against the fugitive in front of him, now heading erratically into Burlington Road and back up in the direction of Leeson Street, Rimmer found himself disconcertingly and vividly in tune with his surroundings, almost as if he had walked this way only yesterday. The clinic on the corner where a great-uncle had breathed his last, the pillar-box in which the duty letter home, scribbled after Commons and posted on the way to the flat, lay awaiting the last collection. Again increasing his pace without appearing appreciably to narrow the distance he began nervously to ransack the future. Perhaps a memorable meal—but where? A Dutch treat? Sheepvart and winkels? But there was nothing on the tongue, the half-conjured Dutch interior itself the thin end of a traveller's tale. Left into Leeson Street. Going in circles. Is he trying to confuse me, gain time to allow the future to fade, strand me in a continuous present, shuffling back to Barbara. *Where did you go? Who was that? Your father?*

Nowhere. Remembered I hadn't posted the letter home. The last connection. They worry, you know. And it was nobody. You imagined it. They're nice. Are they new? Try them on for me, ah, go on.

The sexual image, surely an old man's prurience, momentarily reassured him. Faces, places, names? Dr Kugelkopfschwindel, odd name for an American, in the embassy in Nairobi and his explanation of how he came to be wearing the ribbon of Danelo I of Montenegro. The price of ostrich eggs in Maseru. The souvenir shop in Helsingør with its omelet-prints of . . . none of these, he was sure, came from within his adolescent ambit. His tongue purged rows of intact teeth hoping to tease out a taste of the Tanzanian but, finding nothing, started worrying at the enamel buttress which stood where there should have been a gap in the back row. I want my old body back, farts and all. And the only way is to get back to where I lost it, by the same door as I came out. And to get there first. Abandoning the pursuit Rimmer set off in the direction of a number 8.

12

'The top deck,' said Mr O, 'is for the birds. But there's plenty of room inside. No smoking lower saloon.'

Rimmer had thought at first, from its curious circular radiator glimpsed as it approached him over Ball's Bridge, that it was some kind of service tram, even though he had observed that the wires had disappeared and the remains of the track down to the depot were abandoned. It was only when it came to a juddering halt at the bus stop that he was finally satisfied that it was driven by internal combustion. The driver's seat was on the right, even though it appeared to be a French machine, and Mr O had leant over from behind the steering wheel and the double pair of acytelene headlamps. Without, however, any sign of recognition.

'Or,' he added, 'you could hop up here beside me. You've young legs.'

'Are you heading into town?'

'All the way. A hardy old evening. Watch your step there on the running-board. It's banjaxed.'

As Rimmer grasped one of the supports of the top deck several sets of beady eyes stared down at him.

'Your pigeons . . .'

'They'll come to no harm,' said Mr O, following his gaze. 'Some of them prefer to travel on the roof itself. I was never one for keeping birds in cages.'

'But won't they fly away?'

'Divil a bit. They're trained to stay put until you tie the message onto them. Then, of course, away in a hack. No holding them.'

'But how do you get up to them?' Looking back from the passenger seat into the darkened interior of the vehicle, Rimmer could see no stairs.

'There does be a ladder strapped to the side. A bit hard on the oul' legs. But sure there isn't much call for them these days, not since the postal strike. At that time, no word of a lie, they were comin' from all arts and parts. Down to Findlaters's with an order for a pound of tea. And the oul' wans takin' on when I told them if they thought my birds were goin' to fetch and carry for them they had another think comin'. The Service was the worst, but . . .'

'The service?'

'Up beyond in Merrion Street. Everything in triplicate. It meant three birds at a time, and heaven help me if the carbon got there before the top copy. Then there was your woman wanted to send a postcard to the son in Australia. A postcard! I'm having no bird of mine, sez I, got up like a bleedin' sangwidge man.'

The bus was moving surprisingly smoothly on its solid-tyred wheels, except where it hit a ridge in the stone setts embodying the dead tram-tracks. As they crossed Mount Street Bridge the dingy façades and the few little hucksters' shops were silent and deserted. Later than I thought or perhaps a Sunday evening or a day in the life of someone else altogether.

'Where will I leave you?' asked Mr O as they reached Clare Street.

'College Green, if it's all the same to you. But don't go out of your way.'

'Not a bother. Are you in the College itself?'

'In a manner of speaking. An external student, as you might say.'

'Sure you're better off. I do see them out in the bonafide in Stepaside of a Friday evening. Under the age, the half of them. No manners on any of them. Educated beyond their understanding, as the man said. But that's the Protestants for you. No offence of course.'

'Of course not.'

'A crowd of them up the other night talking nineteen to the dozen about some oul' play they were putting on. *Hamlet*, no less. Oh that this too too sullied flesh . . . that class of thing. And the young ones half out of their . . . well, you wouldn't credit it, expecting to be served pints of porter with the best of them. The boss gave them their comeuppance, no better man. I'll serve you glasses, sez he, as befits your age and station—and sex, if you'll pardon the expression. Didn't put a tooth in it. Janey'—he shivered, swerving inelegantly—'the air bites . . . what's this the way it is?'

'Shrewdly, I think.'

'The very word.' He glanced down at Rimmer's wrist. 'You broke up your watch. It's never that time.'

'It stopped on me. And I've had no trouble with it since I bought it in Weir's, or was it West's, in nineteen fif . . .'

'Nineteen and fifteen? It owes you nothing, so. Though if you were to ask me I would have said it was one of those modern self-winding yokes. Incablocs and all.'

'You're in the watchmaking business?'

'In a manner of speaking, as you put it yourself. I'll let you down here. Mind the step. And look out for that crowd. Angels and ministers for health defend us.'

'I will. And thanks for the lift.'

'Sure you'd have been waiting forever for CIÉ. Good luck now.'

Rimmer stood on the corner of Grafton Street watching the ungainly vehicle take the corner and disappear up Dame Street. The clock on the front of Trinity was showing five to eleven. I come most carefully upon my hour.

13

'Name?' said the porter. A face he didn't recognise. Then or now.

'Rimmer. Number 27.' He couldn't fathom the look of disapproval. Perhaps he should have been on Night Roll? A N Other was standing in the shadows of the deserted Front Gate, shoulders hunched against the chill, studying a poster advertising the Student Christian Movement: *WAS THERE A DOG IN THE MANGER? ALL WELCOME.* 'I've bad news for you,' he said to his back, 'I think we've gained a year or so.'

'I suspected as much. And we've just lost a few hours, according to the porters' clock in the lodge there. How did you get on?'

'Badly.'

'So I see. Still the fresh-faced youth. Though you could do with a shave. You can't go back in that condition.'

'No. Did you see . . .'

'Not a sign. And I've been here some time. The posters are different. *Hamlet.* I seem to recall having had a small part in it. *Hold you your watch tonight? I do, my lord . . .'*

'That's funny. Mr O was on about it.'

'Mr O?'

'He gave me a lift in. But I'll tell you about that some other time. Odd, though, about *Hamlet.*'

'So you said.'

'Fifty-two or fifty-three. You must have graduated. I had.'

'Likewise. But I was hanging on in rooms,' said A N Other, 'in a pretence of doing a Ph.D. Never finished it. Other things . . .'

'You remember the bowler?'

'The what?'

'The dog. Enter Claudius. *Though yet of Hamlet our dear brother's death* and a yelp out of him as some courtier . . .'

'I remember the dog. I was the one stood on the bloody tail.'

'It was mine,' said Rimmer.

'The tail?'

'I was living at home, still looking for a job. Helping out in the office. I used bring him up every night in the da's station wagon. He hated it.'

'The father?'

'Both. I was wasting my time, he said, hanging around the College. Wasn't four years enough for me? And the dog . . .'

'He bit one of the Hamlets. I forget which,' said A N Other. 'They alternated through the week. And sometimes overlapped.'

'I never knew. I used leave him in the care of Osric.'

'Alas poor Osric. I knew him well.'

'I didn't,' said Rimmer. 'And after sitting it out through half of the first night which took four hours I used adjourn to O'Neill's of Suffolk Street. Drank pints. Several pints.'

'The hair of the dog. I'd given up Players. There were too many reluctant graduates like myself around in those times, hanging about months after Mod., pale effulgences of their former selves. But somebody talked me into a walk-on part, Lorenzo or Bernardo or Figaro or someone. Nothing to utter, but at one point I had, according to the producer, to react violently to something Hamlet had to say: *Cans't play upon this pipe? What I, my lord?*

Mimed. The only trouble was that given a choice of three Hamlets on any one night with at least one of the unsuccessful aspirants swelling the *ad hoc* ranks of the courtiers, I never quite knew whom to react to. You know when you walk into a room of black faces not even being able to pick out the man you met in another office half an hour before? They have the same trouble, I believe.'

'And we never met?'

'Two hands, perhaps, patting the same dog,' said A N Other meditatively, 'one in sorrow, one in liquor. No. But then you would never have penetrated my disguise. I was a stickler for the makeup—felt I had to put something into the part to justify all those wasted evenings. I added, at enormous trouble and expense, the Walter Scott beard and high cheekbones, 5 and 9 in all directions . . .'

'I used to overhear bits. One of the Hamlets recorded a soliloquy on tape—a daring innovation for the day—and sat listening to it in dumb amazement, stage right. Especially when the tape stuck and kept on repeating *O God O God O God . . .*'

'*Weary flat stale and . . .*'

'Precisely. Nobody really knew how many O Gods there were meant to be audit, and it must have run on to fifteen before somebody knocked the machine off. Literally. That started off the bloody dog—saving your presence—in the wings. Enter Claudius, pushing the bowler arseways. *It lifted up its head and did address itself to motion, like as it would speak.* Funny how it comes back. *Fie on't fie, 'tis an unseeded garden grown to weeds.* The Hololo Valley . . .'

'Look,' A N Other interrupted. Behind them the porter, unnoticed by either, had been opening the main gate to admit the passage of a motor car. A station wagon. The big black Labrador in the passenger seat obscured their view of the driver.

'I never could keep him in the back. Be arrested nowadays. It must be Himself.' They drew back against the wall as the station wagon passed them, but the passenger gave no sign of recognition. 'He can't go in there like that. And where did he come from?'

'Of course he can. He'll pass for his—your—father, drop the dog and run. Perfectly natural, an old man and his pedigree chum. I seem to recall something of the kind. Will this thing appear again tonight?'

'The poster says so.'

'And Himself would scarcely have brought the dog up otherwise?'

'You're right there, anyway,' said Rimmer. 'A very short fuse, the pater. Took very little to get his beaver up. But it wasn't him. It was me.'

'What was his name?'

'Rimmer, of course. There was nothing irregular about our family, at least not on the surface, which was all that mattered in Newtownmountkennedy.'

'The dog.'

'Mrs Mulligan. Why can I remember the names of dogs but not people?'

'I thought it was a he,' said A N Other, 'at least it always acted like one. I remember before one performance he tried to shag one of the Ophelias.'

'Didn't we all. The sister was a fan of Jimmy O'Dea, Mrs Mulligan the pride of the Coombe who was, of course, a he. But girls took ideas like that in those days, maybe still do. The Mrs didn't catch on though, especially with the dog. So you probably knew him in the attenuated masculine version. But why this sudden interest in canine nomenclature?'

'I've an idea,' said A N Other. 'Come on.'

Rimmer followed dubiously as he headed in the direction of number 4. He felt low. An increasing identification with his youthful body was discounted by a gloomy awareness of the destiny of that firm flesh to thaw and resolve itself into the stew-bloated valetudinarian of the future/present; the stubborn impotence in the loins an untimely reminder of the to-be-incurred debts of the ensemened bed. He half-hoped that A N Other was going to turn right into the jacks and that somehow or other the passage through the airside door would render him once more at one with himself. But he turned left, into the darkened theatre—the actors had not yet come—just as a voice hailed him from the echoing stairway that led up to the spartan rooms surreally illuminated by the changing colours of the Bovril sign on the opposite side of College Green.

'Rimmer! A brilliant paper! A brilliant paper! Your ideas on the recruitment of senior civil servants were most percipient—most percipient!'

How could he explain to the Regius Professor of Economics, now beaming happily at him from the third stair, that it wasn't going to be like that at all? The marks for some exam or other must be just out—even the Prof. was never that indiscreet—or could it have been some term essay? Either way he was totally unprepared. Those machine-gun Little-Go vivas he had never coped with: *Mr Rimmer, how would you prepare a weak solution of NaCl? Mr Rimmer, parse itis apis potanda bigone . . .*

'Thank you, sir.' Lighten the voice. No hint that you will come to know him for a tedious old fool. His three cats, Tibby Laus, Tibby Honor, Tibby . . . no premonition that you're only going to get a second.

'Splendid paper! Splendid paper!'

'Thank you again, sir. Now if you'll excuse me . . .'

'Of course, of course. The play's the thing. A most interesting production, most interesting.'

A N Other was watching anxiously from the darkened doorway to the little theatre, signalling to him with some urgency.

'Of course,' went on Professor Greene, who had prided himself on the breadth of his culture, 'the experiment of multiple casting I do not feel to have been entirely successful. How can two Gertrudes express motherly affection for three different sons? How, we may ask ourselves . . .'

Himself and the dog? Rimmer was wondering as the monologue continued. Then he remembered that he used take him, on the lead of course, for a turn round College Park (the Junior Dean's permission had to be extracted) in the hope of avoiding embarrassing incidents on stage. So presumably . . .

' . . . and lie in the lap of two Ophelias?'

Which was the one O'Flaherty had nicknamed the Helen of Troilism? Another word he had slunk off to look up—and had been unable to find. Wondering on and off down the years whether you'd end up holding your own. But now he had it: this is post-Mod. My paper as visiting speaker, recent graduate of great promise, the Prof. had called me, to the Commerce and Economics Society. Context is all. The memory be green.

'I must go, sir, if you'll excuse me. The dog.'

'Ah yes, of course, Rimmer. The dog-handler, I believe. No gun dog, though, surely? Certainly not last night, oh dear me no. *At the sound it shrunk in haste away.* As must I. Splendid paper, splendid paper.'

As he escaped into the darkness of the theatre A N Other thrust a bundle into his hands.

'Here, get into these. The dressing room's down here.'

'I remember.' He didn't. 'But why?'

'I'll explain later. We must be cap-a-pied before anyone else arrives.'

'And the real cast?'

'The tardy applicants for the positions of gentlemen's gentlemen will just assume that they have been filled on the whim of the producer. Or that space has been found for more favoured friends. Don't put on the light—just in case.'

In the velvety darkness Rimmer wrestled with the unfamiliar tights, the doublet and accoutrements. *No, I am not Lord Hamlet nor was meant to be.* A N Other, remarkably youthful-looking as an emergent courtier, the prudent mouth pursed on a tight, adolescent sneer, the nostrils convex with precocious fastidiousness, the brow ignobly furrowed.

'You haven't . . . ?'

'No danger of that. Come here till I make you up. Your own mother will disown you.'

'To say nothing of the dog. But go easy. Don't forget that I can still see myself, more's the pity.' As A N Other went to work he watched the face in the mirror age into something approximating to his lost identity. There was a commotion somewhere outside.

'Voices,' said Rimmer nervously, 'what do we do now?'

'Retire and time our entrance. Follow me.' A N Other led the way out of the dressing-room just as an agglomeration of students filled the narrow passage. In the semi-darkness they succeeded in evading confrontation, though in the crush Rimmer found himself pressed agreeably up against a young girl. He looked again: Miss Cameron. She, for her part, double-breasted against his accoutrements, was peering up at him in some perplexity.

'Who are *you*? You're dressed early. You're not . . . ?'

But A N Other, fearing that he was about to stand and unfold himself, dragged him by main force through the door. Outside in Front Square a dog barked. Miss Cameron. Must have taken up acting after. But in which case, arriving with Mrs Mulligan, I must surely have bumped into her. Or was this a one-night stand-in? Ophelia, Gertrude . . . ? Surely not. If only I had stayed around, at least once or twice, to see it through.

A N Other, instead of turning right and out into the square, as Rimmer had anticipated, was crossing the hallway, making for the main door of the jacks. His heart lightened again. He's going to try it. But we should have brought our clothes. And what about the overnight bag with all my worldly . . .

'Other, wait! I'll go back and get our things. I'll make some excuse. It might work.'

'It won't. Would you ever hurry up, Rimmer. There's somebody coming.'

They succeeded in getting into the cubicle and bolting the door behind them before the footsteps caught up with them. Nothing seemed to have been disturbed: the inconspicuous bundle was still stuffed behind the porcelain. All that was missing was the airside door. They looked at one another, unable to speak owing to the audible presence in the adjacent cubicle of whoever it was had almost come upon them. Time passed.

And now? grimaced Rimmer eventually, feeling the makeup stretch and resettle.

A N Other's eyes went to heaven under the canopy of his artificed eyebrows. His right hand, opening in a stage gesture, caught Rimmer in the solar plexus. Inadvertently he gasped and loudly broke wind.

Quiet! frowned A N Other, beetling his brows but succeeding, this time, in restraining the hand. He began to mouth silently like a bearer of bad news for the deaf, holding up two bony fingers like a splayed tuning-fork.

'Bean stew,' he apparently said.

'?????,' mimed Rimmer, who was not hungry.

'Bean stew,' A N Other remouthed, indicating with one hand the direction of the theatre and with the other the missing watch which he had scrupulously, in the interests of verisimilitude, left in the dressing-room in his suit pocket.

'?????,' mimed Rimmer again, unable to establish any relationship between these three unknowns.

'Green goo' it looked like this time—an interpretation even less appetising. Then something that resembled 'clean your plate,' again indicating the absent watch. The cubicle began to feel distinctly overcrowded with all these manifestations of anti-matter, particularly since the space restrictions were forcing them to stand close together in what could only be assumed by the partial observer to be a compromising position . . . as indeed it must have looked to the face which appeared over the partition, a face on which vulgar prurience was only marginally modified by its upper containment in a porter's cap.

'Oh my God,' said Rimmer, recognising across the divide the truculent features of Bill Beamish, a porter with whom he had previously shared little in common, and wondering whether makeup and the poor light would save him from the retrospective indignity of being reported to the Junior Dean.

'Bean stew? Green goo? Clean my plate?' he enquired somewhat pettishly of A N Other's doubletted back as he precipitately retreated with him, thankful again for the rejuvenated legs, out of the cubicle, the jacks, and back into the narrow passage of the theatre that led backstage.

'Scene two,' the latter glossed over his shoulder, 'we'll be late.'

'Not our scene, surely?' protested Rimmer, suddenly stage-struck. Their whispered exchange died as from the stage exit immediately in front of them, there stumbled the ghost of Hamlet's father, looking troubled.

'Can't be going too well,' muttered Rimmer, 'your man looks as if he is after muffing his lines.' *It was about to speak when the cock crew,* some muffled oaf was enunciating on stage in the clipped accents of Noel Coward.

'That gives us about five minutes,' said A N Other. 'Horatio winds up the scene, as I remember . . .'

'You remember a lot.'

'Don't forget I had to hang around here night after night, even if it was all of forty years ago, waiting for my insignificant entrance. You must have been well into the third pint. There's the bit about the morn in russet mangle. Then enter king, queen, Hamlet, a few others who escape me and assorted courtiers.'

'Shouldn't we be entering from the dressing-room, with the rest of them?'

'No one will worry. The king was always late, on account of Mulligan. We'll just tag on at the end and position ourselves in watchful and respectful stances around the throne. Do not saw the air with your hand and try to pick somewhere out of the spots.'

'But why?' Rimmer was thinking longingly of his alter ego, or at least its outer lineaments, snug behind a pint in Suffolk Street. What if I were to surprise him, take him suddenly at . . .

A blurry trumpet call sounded, diminished to paper-and-comb timbre by a fibre needle. Horatio and the muffled oaf, exiting unguardedly, became entangled with the advancing procession from the far dressing-room, from which Claudius, dragging a reluctant Mrs Mulligan, was attempting to clear the way. The gramophone stuck on a major third trumpet interval like the yet-to-be-introduced ambulance call, though without the dying fall of the Doppler Effect. As they watched from the shadows Claudius finally succeeded in manoeuvering the dog, tail first, up the two steps to stage level and they heard him, to an obbligato of scrabbling paws and the repeated interval, moving across the stage.

Though yet of Hamlet our dear brother's death . . .

After him shuffled, apparently in no particular order, the rest of the court, the queen at the last moment having been jostled out of the queue by a baby-face Polonius, beard adrift at one corner. Rimmer and A N Other tacked on behind an undifferentiated group of lords, ladies and attendants. It was only when Rimmer, whom Other had meanly edged in front of him, was waiting to put his foot on the first stage step that he realised that he was inhaling from the gowned and wimpled figure in front of him a menstruating Miss Cameron.

Therefore our sometime sister . . . the faint miasma prompted, first, a long-shrouded memory of his Mrs Mulligan sister's dawning womanhood followed by a helter-skelter Fifties olfactory roundup: dusty tram cushions giving way to blackened sausages stuck to the pan in number 27, feet before their weekly immersion in Has Balneas, involuntary semen on unlaundered sheets, Miss Cameron on his knee, the same signal warning him that his hour had not yet come. The tin trumpet, the powder, greasepaint, sweat and excretions closed in on him claustrophobically, trapping him, as it seemed, forever in his callow corporeal frame. With this body thee I never worshipped, Miss Cameron. She shuffled—a shoe loose?—across the stage to take up her position as lefthand maiden to the queen who, Rimmer could now perceive from his frozen attitude with one foot on the stage, was seated on its far side in a huge stone arch like a section of Milltown railway viaduct which, even as he watched, began jerking its way, moved by only too obviously seen hands, in the general direction of a similar construct upon which was seated the king, his fake-jewel-encrusted fingers anxiously patting the head of Mrs Mulligan who had taken up a position with his or her nose buried in the royal genitals.

You, good Cornelius, and you, Voltimand, said Claudius, nervously scanning the assembled courtiers whilst the dog happily snuffled his crotch. The courtiers, with the exception of A N Other and Rimmer, both of whom had secured inconspicuous locations as close to the edge of the action as possible, looked at one another and grinned weakly, reluctant to claim the proffered identities.

Farewell, and let your haste commend your duty, urged the king, a note of uncertainty creeping into his tones. There was an uncomfortable pause, broken only by the sound of the needle skidding across the surface of the trumpet record.

In that, and all things, we will show our duty, suddenly chorused five or six voices as past, present and future bearers of greetings to old Norway decided to opt for early retirement. Four of them made for the exit, one narrowly missing placing a buskined foot on the tail of the dog.

And now, Laertes, what's the news with you? thundered Claudius to the back of the last one, instantly recalling him, no little bewildered, to his duty. *You told us of some suit . . . ?*

A N Other, exhibiting some residual stagecraft and with a lightness in the step that belied his years, had profited from the attempted mass exodus to cross the stage and establish himself beside the still juddering stonework of Queen Gertrude in the plausible role of a second-shift Polonius—a neat enough bit of balancing since the real Polonius, still trying to re-affix his errant beard with one hand (a gesture which lent him the appearance of suffering from acute toothache)—was hovering at a respectful distance from king and dog.

He hath, my lord, wrung from me my slow leave, he intoned from the side of his mouth in an obstinate Tanderagee accent, gesturing at one of the three putative Laerteses with his downstage, non-dental hand.

Take thy fair hour, Laertes, suggested Claudius, hopefully waiting for one of the three to act on the proposition. But the first choice Laertes, having made his brief speech, was going to be denied neither his exit nor the prospect of killing Hamlet, or one of them, some four hours hence. He strode for the wings, casting a suspicious glance at Rimmer almost blocking his way, unsure of what to do with his hands. Anything rather than bring those impetuous fingers into indictable contact with ...

But now, my cousin Hamlet, Claudius continued from a regal arch now is spasmodic motion like a hiccupping gastropod. And *my son,* he added, surveying what remained of his court in the apparent hope of identifying cousin and sibling as two separate entities.

Silence. Two identically-accoutred figures looked at one another.

'Go on, old boy,' muttered one under his British public school breath.

A liddle less than kin ... began the other in a striking, if hesitant Brooklyn accent. At that moment Mrs Mulligan barked.

Whether it was the impact of the encroaching scenery on an extended paw or terminal dissatisfaction with the role assigned him, it was clear that the dog was registering a general rather than a particular protest. His precipitate attempt to withdraw backwards from the sanctum of the king's crotch resulted in Claudius involuntarily losing hold of the leash. Momentarily taken aback at the ease with which he had achieved liberty, Mrs Mulligan turned slowly in his not inconsiderable length, scrutinising the disassembled court as if searching for a familiar face.

And let thine eye look like a friend on Denmark, said Gertrude bravely.

The dog's ears went up, the nose twitched. The heavy paws flexed with agility and with a wag of the tail that dashed a wine goblet, full, from the king's fingers he bounded across the stage towards Rimmer.

There seemed little option but to turn and run.

14

'You'd miss the bus, though,' said Mr O.

'I thought this was destined for the museum,' said A N Other.

'And so it was. But sure there was some mixup about premises—at the heel of the hunt they couldn't get the insurance, or whatever. So I'm after volunteering to look after her and keep her in running order. At my own expense, I don't mind telling you. Until they can come up with something. It's costing me a fortune in birdseed but . . .'

The chase had been short and sharp. Even Rimmer's rejuvenated legs had been no match for Mrs Mulligan in full flight. He had cleared the stage steps, the passage and the theatre door with a slight lead, but the dog had caught up with him as he headed wildly down across Front Square in the direction of the Rubrics. He ran with no clear intention—except, perhaps, that of taking refuge in the rooms in number 27—but as he made for the staircase he had collided with a figure emerging from the doorway. When he recovered himself he realised that the dog had transferred his attentions to the stranger, who had fallen back against the brickwork trying to fend him off. Rimmer turned and made off along the path to the Campanile in the direction of Front Gate, but his legs were heavy, his breathing laboured even allowing for the effects of the 200 metres sprint. He had almost collapsed into the arms of A N Other who had emerged from the shadows of the doorway of number 5.

'Clothes,' he said briefly, pressing an untidy bundle into Rimmer's hands. 'Come on.'

'Where? The jacks?'

'Too risky. They've announced an interval to get themselves sorted out. The jacks will be full of incontinent audience. We must get out of this gear. An empty room. Leave the makeup, it may serve to confuse the pursuit. If any.'

And it was thus that they had contrived to stroll nonchalantly through Front Gate, Rimmer with a feeling of heaviness as after an undigested meal.

'Lucky I was passing,' said Mr O. 'Did you enjoy the play-acting?'

'In a manner of speaking,' said Rimmer.

'Never had any time for it meself. Living on immoral yearnings, as the man said. Stick to the business of being yourself. This day and age.'

'Where are we going?' asked Rimmer.

'Home, where else? The last run of the day. Even birds has to sleep. You'll join me in a jar, gentlemen?'

'The bonafide?'

'Hop in. The pair of yous'll be more comfortable inside.'

They walked to the rear entrance. The interior of the vehicle was a jumble, a random selection from a garden shed. There was a flurry in the pigeon-cotes above them as the driver threw the machine into a coruscating first gear.

'Oh and there was a message,' he said, leaning back through a partition from which a pane of glass had been removed, 'the last one in. Cute as a Cappoquin chicken—wouldn't come near me till I rattled the bag of birdseed.'

A N Other took the metal cylinder and unwrapped a telex form: *ATTENTION PAX STOP THIS IS IMPORTANT STOP SOAP OF THE DAYS STOP FARCED PIGGIN A LA FRANCES STOP EMITS TWO AIRSIDE.*

'But I can't,' said Rimmer, 'not like this. You'll have to eat for both of us.'

'It says two,' insisted A N Other. 'Take off your makeup.' It sounded almost a sexual suggestion. Picking up from the littered floor a page of the *Times Pictorial: THREE TRAMS WITH NO PLACE TO GO,* Rimmer began scrubbing at the heavy layer of makeup. It hurt.

'Look at yourself,' suggested A N Other.

The dusty windows of the mobile pigeon-cotes acted as a mirror in which he could see reflected the assembled contents of the interior. Not, however, himself.

'You see?' said A N Other, working on his own makeup. As he removed eyebrows, beard and thickly-applied 5 and 9 the reflected lineaments of his face progressively dissolved.

'I don't understand,' said Rimmer.

'That character you ran into in your race with Mulligan—Himself. The impact must have knocked the stuffing out of him.'

Rimmer patted his restored paunch appreciatively. 'I'm not really sorry to lose the legs.' He stretched his ageing limbs experimentally, grimacing at the familiar twinge of arthritis. 'Nor the hands—apart from the piano.' He held them up.

'I swear to God they were all set to rummage your woman.'

'I married her, you know,' said A N Other flatly.

'You mean . . . ?'

'Miss Cameron. I suppose I owe you an apology.'

'And how is the present Mrs Other?'

'Someone altogether different. It didn't work out.'

'I'm sorry.'

'You have no cause to be. I met her long after College, on a trip home. Impulse buying, I think, on both sides. I owe you an apology.'

'You do not. It never amounted to anything. Puppy-love. Though that bastard at the party . . .'

'I saw him too. But I still owe you an apology.'

'I've told you: forget it.'

'That thing about the play. My motives were purely selfish. I didn't really think it would help to get us back. I wanted another look at her, close up, being herself. I wanted to see her . . . you know . . . I've lived a rather sheltered life, Rimmer. It seemed, in the safety of another time, a chance to . . .'

'What were you proposing? Rape in front of Mrs Mulligan? She was having a period.'

'I don't know much about animals.'

The mobile pigeon-cote jolted to a halt at a traffic light.

'Where are we?' asked A N Other.

Rimmer scrubbed at the mottled glass. 'No idea. More important—when are we?'

A N Other was scrutinising what was left of the *Times Pictorial*. 'It looks like March 4, 1950. Though that last figure could be a 2 or a 3 or a 9. Does it matter?'

'Not really. I've lost my curiosity about the past. Kid's stuff. Hindsight is overrated. I'll take what's left to me as it comes.'

The vehicle stopped again. A N Other in turn started rubbing at the window. 'We're still in the city? Surely?'

Mr O turned and put his head through the missing panel. 'I'll let yez down here, lads, and open the door for you. The switch is on the right as you go in. Mind the step. I have to park the yoke beyond.'

Rimmer and A N Other found themselves in a dingily-lit city street in front of a small shop which, to judge by the haphazard display in the darkened window, was either a pawnbroker or a modest jewellery establishment or both. Mr O had left the engine running and was back in the driver's seat before they had reached the door. Rimmer entered the premises cautiously, feeling along the wall for the switch. The door to the shop proper, unlocked, was on their left. Ahead was another door, apparently leading to living or other domestic quarters.

'Better wait here I suppose,' said A N Other, opening the shop door and switching on another light inside.

There was little in the place to command attention. A wooden counter surmounted by a few showcases holding Monopol watch straps, Hollywood fashion jewellery. A mounted showcard issued by the Rolex Watch Company of Switzerland carried the information that the precision of a watch depends to a great extent upon the accurate functions of the balance and hairspring. *With each 'tic-tac' the balance wheel performs a complete oscillation with the following interesting results.*

'I doubt it,' said Rimmer.

'Why are all the clocks saying the same time?' asked a voice.

Neither of them had been aware of the small girl, clutching a battered copy of *Ciarán the Compatible Mouse* in one grubby hand and an equally battered wrist-watch in the other, who had followed them in and was now staring up at the wall behind the counter where an array of clocks and watches of various shapes and sizes was displayed.

'They all have their hands in the air,' she said, 'as if they were cheering. But I think they're all stopped. How did they all stop at the same time, mister? And in the dark? I don't want the clocks to stop in the dark.'

'It's the way they make them,' said A N Other. 'The people who make the clocks put the hands at ten to ten because they think it looks nice. Ten to ten is past your bedtime, isn't it?'

'In Africa some beleaguered parrots go to bed about ten to ten,' said Rimmer, 'did you know that?'

'Ciarán the 'patible mouse doesn't. Nor does my da. He's still in the pub. He comes home *much* later. Only now he can't tell what time it is because his watch is broke. Can you mend it, mister? Can you?'

'The real shop man isn't here,' said Rimmer. 'And anyway it's too late. You should be in bed. What's your name?'

'Barbara. What time is it? Really and truly?'

'Both our watches are broken too,' said A N Other. 'We saw the light on and came in to see could we get them mended. Like you. But there's nobody here. On the other hand . . .'

'My da's only needs one. The little one won't go round without the big one.'

'I don't know what the man does with his hands,' said A N Other. 'But there might be some out the back. If you wait here my friend and I will go and have a look. Come on, Rimmer.'

'I saw a funny bus. The downstairs was full of feathers.'

'It's one of those things that transports you back in time. Come on, Rimmer.'

'But . . .'

'Come *on*!' He opened a small door at the back of the shop. 'There must be one out here somewhere.'

'A hand?'

'A jacks. It might be our only chance.'

'But remember what you said about going out the same door that . . .'

'Never mind that. Look.'

The jacks was surprisingly capacious, containing not only a filthy wash-hand-basin but, in the adjacent wall, another door.

'Gentlemen'—the voice of Mr O came from the shop behind them:

'Would you ever give this little lady a big . . .'

'After you,' said A N Other.

15

Kevin Ndegwa was reading, slowly and for the third time, page 18 of 'Scouts and Human Settlements.' *Using mortar mesh technology. Striking the Shutters,* he read: *Depending upon weather conditions, the removal of the shutter can commence after 3 to 4 days. If for practical reasons you wish to leave the shutters in position for longer you may do so without any difficulties arising. When removing or 'striking' the shutters, <u>first remove all temporary nailing</u>, bracing timbers, etc. <u>Avoid placing too much stress on the mortar.</u>* All that he understood, as well as what followed about repeated gentle shaking and pulling gradually loosening the first shutter, and making good any small irregularities or imperfections with a wet mortar mix. He had seen these things demonstrated at the scout headquarters in Nairobi. The wall plates had been cast into the mortar mesh wall at an angle, ready to receive the corrugated iron roofing sheets which were stacked in a neat pile ready for fixing. All this was fine. The only thing that bothered him was the first sentence: *Depending on the weather conditions . . .* He looked up at the unchanging blue sky. It was a warm, but not too warm day. He could not remember the last rain. Were these the conditions to depend on? He tried to think of a practical reason for leaving the shutters in position for longer but the only practical reason he could think of was the weather conditions. He flipped over the pages in the hope of finding the answer buried somewhere in the list of equipment *(5–10 shovels, 3–5 saws, 5–10 jembes, 3–4 wheelbarrows, 1 tamper).* How did one tamper? He had forgotten that piece of information but perhaps he had done it without knowing, as he was going to have to cease to depend upon the weather conditions. He turned on to the drawings on page 27, remembered how he had thought that the plan of the building, when he first saw it, looked like two elephants back to back, the he-elephant and the she-elephant. VIP. Ventilated improved pit. These buildings attracted words like flies. He picked up his nail bar just as two white men emerged from the female elephant side.

'Jambo,' said the first, thinner one. 'Your work is good. It will be the pride of the village.'

Kevin was puzzled. He knew neither of the men, though he still found it difficult to remember one white face from another over any length of time. He had not seen them arrive but, he reflected, nor had he seen them not arrive. He had certainly not seen them go into his unfinished VIP latrine.

The smaller, fatter one was sweating inside what looked like a coat made from a heavy blanket. He seemed unhappy.

'What is the name of this *kijiji*?' he asked in a manner which told Kevin Ndegwa that he knew nothing. He told him.

'And this is your first VIP latrine?'

'Yes, sir.' He thought it better to be polite until he found out what the men wanted.

'No other latrine at all?' said the thinner man.

'Just this. Mortar mesh technology, sir. The government of Ireland . . .'

'Yes, I know.' The thin one also sounded worried. 'How far is the next *kijiji*?'

'Perhaps half a day. Where did you put your truck? I did not hear you coming.'

'Never mind,' said the fat one, 'let's just complete the inspection, shall we? If you don't mind.'

'I don't mind,' said Kevin, 'but you must be careful of the walls. I was about to commence the removal of the shutters. Depending, of course, on the weather conditions. Perhaps you could advise me if I can depend . . .'

'Of course, of course,' the thinner one interrupted rudely. 'You may commence just as soon as we have completed our inspection. This side now, I think, Rimmer . . .'

The two of them disappeared into the male elephant side. Kevin Ndegwa heard voices, apparently arguing, and hoped that they were not, whoever they were, finding fault with his workmanship. Then silence. He waited politely, flicking through the pages of the instruction book: *Alternatively if putty is not available or unnecessary a second slip can be used to hold the glass in position.* Putty was not available, although it had been promised; nor, of course, in a VIP latrine was it necessary, or even desirable. The sun was sinking. Soon, he thought, the weather conditions will not be dependable. He picked up the nail board again, deciding to explain as politely as possible that it was now three to four days and for practical reasons he did not wish to leave the shutters in position for longer.

He was surprised, but not very surprised, to find no one in the male elephant side of the latrine. Just to be sure he looked also in the female elephant side, but there was nothing there but a crumpled piece of paper which he recognised as a telex message but which was made up of words he could not understand. He smoothed it out and speared it, with a feeling of modest satisfaction, on a protruding nail.

SELECTED DALKEY ARCHIVE PAPERBACKS

FOR A FULL LIST OF PUBLICATIONS, VISIT:
www.dalkeyarchive.com

SELECTED DALKEY ARCHIVE PAPERBACKS